THE
SPRITE
SISTERS

THE
SPRITE
SISTERS

NEW MAGIC

SHERIDAN WINN

PICCADILLY PRESS · LONDON

The Sprite Sisters series

The Circle of Power
The Magic Unfolds
The Secret of the Towers
The Ghost in the Tower
New Magic

First published in Great Britain in 2010
by Piccadilly Press Ltd,
5 Castle Road, London NW1 8PR
www.piccadillypress.co.uk

A catalogue record for this book is available
from the British Library.

ISBN: 978 1 84812 056 3 (paperback)

Printed and bound in Great Britain by CPI Bookmarque Ltd
Cover design by Simon Davis
Cover illustration by Sue Hellard
Sprite Towers map by Chris Winn

Mixed Sources
Product group from well-managed
forests and other controlled sources
www.fsc.org Cert no. TT-COC-002227
© 1996 Forest Stewardship Council
FSC

For Mandy,
who's been very brave

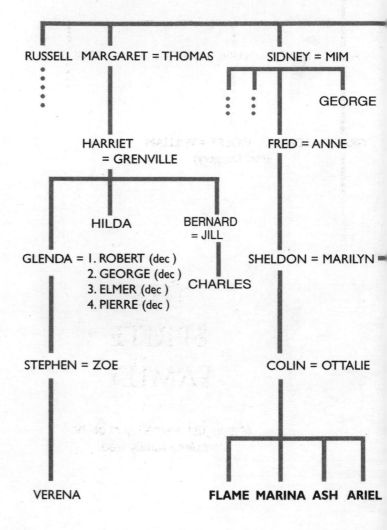

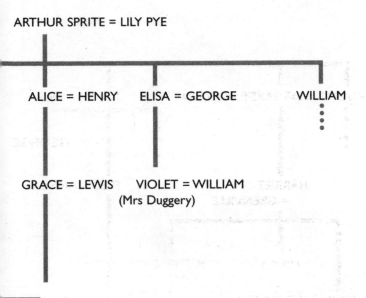

ARTHUR SPRITE = LILY PYE

ALICE = HENRY   ELISA = GEORGE   WILLIAM

GRACE = LEWIS   VIOLET = WILLIAM
                  (Mrs Duggery)

THE
SPRITE
FAMILY

This is just a small part of the
complete family tree.

THE CIRCLE OF POWER

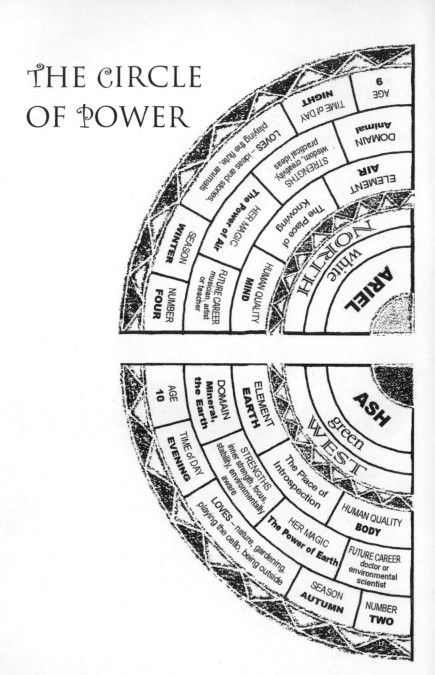

AGE 6

TIME of DAY NIGHT

DOMAIN Animal

ELEMENT AIR

STRENGTHS wisdom, creativity, practical ideas

LOVES – ideas and stories, playing the flute, animals

The Power of Air

HER MAGIC

The Place of Knowing

SEASON WINTER

FUTURE CAREER musician, artist or teacher

HUMAN QUALITY MIND

NUMBER FOUR

NORTH

white

ARIEL

ELEMENT EARTH

DOMAIN Mineral, the Earth

AGE 10

TIME of DAY EVENING

STRENGTHS inner strength, focus, stability, environmentally aware

The Place of Introspection

LOVES – nature, gardening, playing the cello, being outside

The Power of Earth

HER MAGIC

HUMAN QUALITY BODY

FUTURE CAREER doctor or environmental scientist

SEASON AUTUMN

NUMBER TWO

ASH

green

WEST

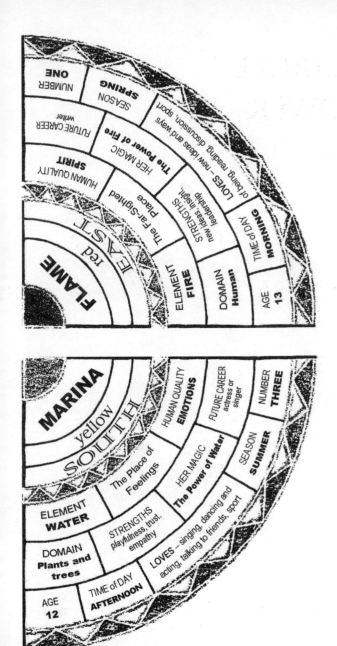

FLAME
red EAST
NUMBER ONE
SEASON SPRING
FUTURE CAREER writer
HER MAGIC The Power of Fire
HUMAN QUALITY SPIRIT
The Far-Sighted Place
STRENGTHS new ideas, insight, leadership
LOVES – new ideas and ways of being, reading, discussion, sport
ELEMENT FIRE
DOMAIN Human
TIME of DAY MORNING
AGE 13

MARINA
yellow SOUTH
HUMAN QUALITY EMOTIONS
FUTURE CAREER actress or singer
NUMBER THREE
The Place of Feelings
HER MAGIC The Power of Water
SEASON SUMMER
ELEMENT WATER
STRENGTHS playfulness, trust, empathy
LOVES – singing, dancing and acting, talking to friends, sport
DOMAIN Plants and trees
AGE 12
TIME of DAY AFTERNOON

CHAPTER ONE

VERENA'S HANDS

VERENA GLASS held out her long, slim hands. Why were they feeling so tingly? What was this strange sensation coursing through her fingers? She'd never felt it before. It's like electricity, she thought, staring at her palms. She turned her hands over. They looked the same as usual – soft, pink skin and short, carefully filed nails – but something felt different.

She looked out of her bedroom window across the undulating countryside of north Norfolk. The fields around The Oaks were winter brown and the trees bare. A flurry of snowflakes fell past the window. She shivered slightly. Despite its elegant furnishings, the big house felt empty and cold. There's been no laughter here since my mother left, she thought, sitting back against her iron bedstead.

Her thoughts turned to Sprite Towers, a mile down the road. There would be hustle and bustle today in the big, warm kitchen, as the Sprite family prepared for Christmas. I wonder what Flame and her sisters are doing? I'll bet they're having fun.

It's the twelfth of December today, so only thirteen days now till Christmas, she thought, smiling to herself. Mummy will be home in a few days. Not long to wait. I've missed her so much.

Whoosh! Another burst of energy surged through her fingers. She drew a sharp breath and stared down at her hands again. What's happening? What does it mean, she wondered.

From downstairs in the hallway, she heard her grand-mother call up the stairs. 'Lunchtime!'

Verena's mouth tightened and she gave a heavy sigh. I'm not going to say anything to Grandma about my hands, she thought.

But there was no hiding from Glenda Glass. As soon as they sat down at the table, Verena felt her grandmother watching her closely. Several times as they ate their meal, Verena caught her glance. Each time, Glenda turned away instantly.

She knows something has happened, thought Verena. I can feel it. It's as if she sees straight through me – but I won't say anything.

Glenda ate quietly and precisely, her back straight, her head perfectly angled. A ballet dancer in her youth, she still moved elegantly and freely. 'What have you been doing?' she asked.

'Just messing about in my room,' replied Verena.

'You seem a little anxious,' Glenda commented.

'I was thinking about Mummy,' replied Verena, quickly.

'She'll be home soon,' said Glenda, with a small smile – so small that Verena was reminded that having Zoe home was the last thing her grandmother wanted. It was Glenda who had broken her parents' marriage and driven her mother away. Verena had learned that a few weeks ago, when she overheard her distant Sprite cousin, Charles Smythson, arguing with her grandmother. It was then that she heard them talk about the 'magic power' of the Sprite family – and that Glenda had misused her power.

What it all meant, Verena did not know. She had asked Flame Sprite about magic power, but the other girl would say nothing – nor would her sister, Marina, when she asked her. All Flame would tell her was that she would understand when the time came. When what time came, she had wondered. Still, she consoled herself, at least Flame listened to me. It was the first time we have ever really talked.

She thought about asking her grandmother about magic power, but Glenda frightened her. If what Charles had said was true, then her grandmother was someone to be feared, not trusted.

Instinctively Verena knew he was right: there had been so many occasions over the last few months when Glenda had pressed her – bullied her – for information on the Sprites. She had noticed that Glenda's cold blue eyes took on a glacial look and her thin mouth tightened whenever the sisters or their grandmother, Marilyn, were mentioned.

None of the Sprites like her – that's clear to see, she thought. I wonder what's really going on?

Conscious of Glenda's scrutiny, Verena tried to concentrate on the plate of roast chicken and vegetables in front of her. 'Nice lunch, Grandma – thank you,' she murmured.

'Thank *you*,' said Glenda, slightly taken aback. Verena rarely commented on her cooking.

They ate in silence for a little while, then Glenda asked once more, 'Are you sure you're feeling okay? You look a little shaky.'

'Yes – I'm fine,' said Verena, swallowing a mouthful of roast potato and gripping her knife and fork tightly.

Grandma *is* looking at my hands, she thought. Can she *see* what is happening to me? Should I say something?

For a second she deliberated. It would be so nice to talk to someone – but something in the back of her mind said, 'Say nothing.' So the meal continued, largely silent.

As soon as she had helped her grandmother clear away the lunch things, Verena dashed back up to her bedroom. Just as she was safely in, *whoosh* went the feeling again, as the sensation of electricity surged through her hands. She stood against the closed door, her heart pounding.

I must call Flame, she thought, moving across the room and grabbing her mobile. Sitting down heavily on her bed, she jabbed Flame's number on the keypad – and waited.

'Flame, something weird is happening to me! My grandmother has seen it, but I don't know what it is!' she wanted to say – but there was no answer and eventually the voicemail clicked in. Verena stared across the room. I can't tell Flame this in a message, she thought.

Whoosh! A much stronger bolt of energy surged through her hands, this time going right up her arms. Verena cried out in shock and sat, panting, on the bed.

Keep calm, she thought. Breathe deeply and slowly. Look out at the trees.

For almost a minute she sat there, perfectly still, until her mind cleared and her body relaxed. Then she focused her thoughts on the feeling in her hand, drew a deep breath and raised her right arm so that it was level with her shoulder. Holding her arm steady, she curled her thumb and fingers into the palm of her hand and pointed her index finger straight.

She waited. The tingling feeling grew stronger – then died away.

This is silly, she thought, bending her hand towards her and looking at her index finger. She smiled to herself. What am I doing? What do I expect to happen?

She lowered her hand and looked around the room. Outside, the afternoon light was dimming. Soon be time to turn on the lights, she thought.

She sat back against her pillows and leaned her left hand on the iron bedpost.

Then, as if by some instinct, she lifted her right hand and pointed her finger at the light bulb that hung from the middle of the ceiling in the centre of a cerise lampshade.

Once more, this time stronger than before, the surge of feeling whooshed down her arm. It shot through her hand and out of her finger – and the light bulb lit up. At the same time, the light switch on the wall went down with a click.

Verena cried out in surprise and lowered her hand. She stared up at the light in amazement. 'Oh my God! What have I done? Did I do that?' she said out loud.

There was a knock at the bedroom door. Glenda Glass opened it and put her head around. 'Is everything all right, Verena?' she asked. 'I thought I heard you cry out.'

'I had a bit of tummy ache,' said Verena, quickly. 'I'm just lying down for a little while.'

Glenda cast her eyes around the room – glanced up at the glowing ceiling light – then focused on Verena. Glenda's cold blue eyes seemed to bore a hole through her.

'I'm all right, Grandma,' she said, quickly. 'I'll be down in a little while. Perhaps we could watch a film together?'

Glenda nodded. 'All right. See you downstairs,' she said and left the room, shutting the door behind her.

Verena listened as her grandmother descended the stairs. Then she got off the bed and quietly opened the bedroom door a crack. She could hear her grandmother moving about downstairs. All safe, she thought, shutting the door quietly and returning to her bed.

Sitting down on the bed, she grabbed the iron bedstead with her left hand and pointed her right index finger up at the light bulb hanging from the ceiling. This time she expected the feeling to surge through her hand. And it did. *Bing!* The bulb went off – and the switch on the wall clicked back up.

She tried again – and the light bulb lit up. Then she turned it off. On, off, on, off, she thought, as she started to tune her mind to what the light bulb was doing.

For the next few minutes, in the gathering dark of her room, Verena Glass played with this new ability. Then she pushed back her long blond hair and stared at her index finger, wiggled it about and turned it around.

I can make a light go on or off by holding out my finger and thinking. It's amazing! It's like some kind of magic power, she thought.

Then she sat still for a moment, stared again at her hand. Is that what I have, she wondered. A magic power? I *am* a Sprite – and I overheard Charles say to Grandma that some Sprites have magic power. Is this what Flame and her sisters have? Do they light up things?

Perhaps that's why neither Flame nor Marina would speak about it, she thought. If they hadn't got magic power, they'd have laughed at me and told me I was silly. But they didn't. They both looked at me as if I was suddenly very interesting – as if there was something new they had seen in me.

Oh my goodness, she thought with a smile. Perhaps I am a magic Sprite!

But it seems as if there are different types of magic, she thought. She cast her mind back to the argument she had overheard between her grandmother and Charles. He had told her she was a 'despicable human being', who hurt people without any regard for the consequences. He said she had used her magic power to hurt the Sprites and had tried to steal Sprite Towers. He even said she had stolen Marilyn Sprite's money!

If that's true, no wonder the Sprite family don't like her, thought Verena. What would Grandma do if she knew I had power, too? Would she be pleased? Or would she be angry? Would she make me hurt the Sprite Sisters?

Verena sat up on the bed. I must talk to Flame as soon as I can – but I must not say anything to Grandma, she thought. I must *not* let her know what's happened. She scares me enough anyway, without her knowing this.

At that moment, she heard her grandmother calling her. 'Verena, are you coming down?'

'Coming now,' shouted Verena, and she got off the bed and walked towards the door.

At Sprite Towers, there had indeed been hustle and bustle that day – and not just in the kitchen. Whilst Grandma and Flame iced the Christmas cake on the kitchen table, Marina, Ash and Ariel were helping their mother to decorate the Christmas tree. The huge Norway Spruce standing in the corner of the drawing room was already covered in an array of lights and coloured baubles.

Bert, Grandma's sausage dog, lay by the blazing log fire and looked on. His long floppy ears hung over his face as he rested his head on his front legs.

'Right, that's enough,' said Mum, picking up Archie, the seventeen-week-old black Labrador puppy who was sniffing around the wire of the fairy lights. Apart from getting under everybody's feet and chewing various decorations, he had already done a pee behind the sofa. Mum marched off to the kitchen with him under her arm and came back without him, shutting the door behind her.

Now, while the girls worked on the tree, Mum turned

her attention to the Christmas cards. First she attached the cards to wide red ribbons. Then she climbed up the stepladder and hung the ribbons from the picture rail that ran right around the wall, close to the high ceiling. There were so many paintings and Sprite family portraits on the walls that there was little space for cards, but Mum managed to fit them all in.

'There'll be more to come,' said Marina, looking up.

'We can hang them either side of the fire,' said Mum.

The drawing room was the most elegant room in the house, with its high ceiling and duck egg blue walls, the carved stone fireplace and the huge oak bookcase that covered the west wall. Because of its size, and the expense of heating the room, the Sprites used it only on special occasions. Christmas was always one of them. It was here, sitting on the cream sofas and the Persian rugs that covered the polished oak floor, that everyone would open their presents on Christmas Day.

By early afternoon, the tree was finished.

'That looks festive!' said Dad, as he wandered into the drawing room. He had been working at home in his office, at the side of the house, that day.

'It's all sparkly!' said Ariel. Her big grey eyes shone with delight.

'Certainly is!' agreed Dad, putting his arm around her shoulders.

Ash came up to her father and gave him a hug. They were especially close – partly from a shared love of being in the garden and growing things and partly because they were both quiet people.

'You've all done a grand job,' said Dad. 'We're going to have a wonderful Christmas.'

CHAPTER TWO

FLAME NEEDS
TO THINK

AS SOON as everything was cleared up in the kitchen, Flame went up to her bedroom. She had enjoyed decorating the Christmas cake and the general family cheer, but now she wanted to be alone.

Flame needed to think – and she needed to check something.

The eldest of the Sprite Sisters, she was the one with the gift of being able to see ahead. Part of her power of the east was her far-sightedness. If the sisters were in danger, it was usually Flame who found a way out.

A few weeks ago, around Hallowe'en, an evil ghost had haunted Sprite Towers. It wasn't any old ghost who had roamed the corridors and scared everyone witless. This ghost was the spirit of Glenda Glass's grandmother, Margaret.

It was Flame's ability to see the future and to form a good plan that had enabled the sisters to remove the ghost from the house. True, the eldest Sprite Sister had a bit of a temper, but she had courage and she was determined. Most of all, she was very protective of her sisters.

Something had been bothering Flame all day. She was not sure yet what it was. Just one of her 'feelings', as her sisters would say. This feeling was new. Since late morning, her right hand and arm had been tingling.

Now, as she closed her bedroom door behind her, the tingling increased. A pulse of energy seemed to move down her arm. But this wasn't like the feeling of her own power, the power of Fire. No, this was different.

Why does Verena Glass's face keep coming into my mind? Are these things connected, Flame wondered, as she moved across to the bookshelves on the far side of her room.

Kneeling down on the navy blue carpet, she leaned forward and pulled out some of the large books on the bottom shelf. Behind these, tucked up against the corner, was a small wooden box shaped like an old-fashioned cigar box.

Flame lifted the box from its hiding place and laid it on her lap. For a few seconds she lingered, tracing her finger around the pattern etched in the wood. The design was the shape of a circle, crossed through twice.

The Crossed Circle, she remembered. Mrs Duggery told us to watch for it. She said there was treasure to be found in Sprite Towers. She thought of the tiny, very old lady with her lilac knitted hat and her big brown boots. Mrs Duggery had the most powerful magic of all the Sprites. Even Glenda Glass, with her dark power, was no match for Mrs Duggery.

We've been so busy with all the pre-Christmas paraphernalia that we'd forgotten about the treasure, thought Flame, as she prised open the lid of the box. I must talk to my sisters – and we must start looking for the Crossed Circle. We need to find this 'treasure', whatever it is. Glenda Glass has been quiet since the ghost went away, but for how long? We're never safe with her about, using her dark magic against us.

Flame looked into the open wooden box. Inside were four dried, rather frail rosebuds, two old black and white family photographs, a little key, an envelope addressed to the Sprite Sisters with a letter inside, and a thick piece of paper, folded twice.

Flame lifted out the folded paper, closed the lid and rested the box down on the floor. Leaning back against the bookshelves, she opened the paper and cast her eyes over it. She had studied this piece of paper a hundred times and knew every mark and detail.

Drawn in black ink and written in an old-fashioned hand were the section plans of each floor of Sprite Towers, from the ground floor to the attics on the third floor and the two towers. On each floor plan was the wide staircase that wound up through the centre of the house, connecting the bottom to the top.

The plan sections were covered in a variety of small ink marks, including the letters *E*, *S*, *W* and *N*. It was these letters – representing east, south, west and north – that the Sprite Sisters followed to create the magic that opened the portal.

This piece of paper is priceless, thought Flame. Glenda Glass would stop at nothing to get her hands on the secret plan of Sprite Towers, which enabled us to open the portal to travel back in Sprite family time. And George Sprite – he told us to watch the plan. Flame remembered the meeting with their long-dead great-great-great uncle, who travelled through the portal to see them. I must look at it carefully, she thought.

As Flame stared at the plan, she became aware of a nagging feeling in the back of her mind. It was something George had said, when he came to warn them about Margaret Sprite. '*A time will come when the marks on the secret plan will change*,' he had said. There was more we had to learn, she remembered, and we would know what to do when the time came.

So has the time come, she wondered. She studied the plan carefully, but none of the marks had changed, as far as she could see. But somewhere in the back of her mind she had the sense that something was different.

Something is going to happen – or it is already happening, she thought, biting her lip. I can feel it. And this strange sense of tingling in my right arm and hand: what does that mean?

Again, Verena Glass's face came into her mind. She had the feeling there was something she wanted to tell her. Verena had been her hated rival at school: the girl who was quick to put Flame down at any opportunity, the distant Sprite cousin and granddaughter of Glenda Glass.

What is changing, wondered Flame.

She put down the box and walked over to her bedside cupboard. There, beside the lamp, was her mobile phone.

There was a missed call, she noticed: Verena's number.

Verena called me – only a little while ago – but did not leave me a message, she thought. I wonder what she wants to tell me? Shall I call her?

Flame walked to the window and stared out over the grounds of Sprite Towers. The sky looked dark and heavy with snow. Down by the stables, she could see Dad and Ash loading logs on to the trailer of the little tractor, to bring them up to the house. Archie was running round in circles on the lawn, carrying a big stick.

She pushed her thick copper-coloured hair back from her face, noticed a few snowflakes float past.

Ever since the Hallowe'en party, things have changed between Verena and me, she thought. Up till then, I'd refused to have anything to do with her. Her friendship with Marina had caused problems between us sisters. Then there's Quinn, who I thought liked me, but who also seems to like Verena. That hasn't helped. But at the party, when I saw the ghost of Margaret Sprite swirling around her, and I saw Verena wasn't frightened, something happened.

All the other girls had been petrified, but not her, thought Flame. Verena was fascinated by the ghost of her great-great-grandmother – and she *knew* I was watching her. Something changed in that moment. Maybe seeing her like that sparked a new feeling of respect.

But it was more than that, thought Flame. It was a sense: a sense that Verena may have the magic power that runs through the family, although she didn't know it.

She stood completely still, her eyes wide, though staring

into space. Her breathing quickened as an insight rippled through her mind.

I know what Verena wants to tell me, she thought. I bet she's found her power! But why would she get it now? We Sprite Sisters got our power on our ninth birthdays – and so did Grandma.

Flame could think of no answer for this question. Maybe Glenda was older when she got her magic, she considered. Maybe the coming of the power follows a different route in different parts of the family.

Now what, she wondered. Will Glenda find out – and if so, what will she do? Will she try to turn Verena against us and cause us further harm – or should we help Verena and try to protect her from her grandmother?

Flame turned on the lamp and went back to the wooden box on the carpet. She picked up the plan and looked at it.

Something was different. She could sense it before she saw it.

I'm sure that dot wasn't there a little while ago, she thought, peering hard at a small black mark that had appeared in the centre of the West Tower.

Flame shivered with excitement. I must tell my sisters, she thought. And maybe they'll have some thoughts on Verena, as well.

Flame folded up the plan and put it back in the box. She tucked this into the corner of the shelf and put back the large books in front of it to hide it. Her grandmother, Marilyn, knew of its existence, but the Sprite Sisters had never mentioned it to their parents. Neither their mother nor their father had any

16

idea of their magic powers. Although Dad was a Sprite, he had not inherited the magic power. He'd heard about it, of course, but it was never discussed. The girls only ever talked about their power to their grandmother. She always told them they must keep it secret or it would weaken.

Mum and Dad knew nothing about the dark magic Glenda Glass had used against the family since her arrival in the village in early June. Nor did they know the truth about Mrs Duggery. Mum would never have believed them anyway, Flame knew. Despite Mum's experience with the ghost, she dismissed the notion of anything supernatural. Dad was more open-minded. He had seen and felt the ghost at Sprite Towers and knew it was real, whereas Mum had blanked it from her mind as soon as it was gone.

George Sprite told us to guard the secret plan with our lives, thought Flame. If Glenda Glass got hold of it, she would use it to hurt us. But I wonder what Mum would do with it, if she ever found it? She'd probably say it was all nonsense.

Flame cast her eyes around the room. The plan is safe here, she thought. I'll keep an even closer eye on it, now that the marks are starting to change.

Now, what shall I do about contacting Verena, she wondered, as she shut her bedroom door and walked along the corridor. But as she came down the staircase, she heard Marina calling up. 'Flame! Flame!'

Flame started to run down. 'What's happened?' she asked, meeting Marina halfway and seeing her tense face.

'Verena's mum's had a riding accident!' said Marina. 'Mum and Dad have just got a call from her father and they're talking to him now. He's flying straight out to Buenos Aires to be with her. Apparently, she's broken her collar bone and some ribs and may have punctured a lung. The doctors are not sure she'll be able to travel home before Christmas.'

'Oh my goodness!' said Flame. 'Poor Zoe! And Verena – she'll be so upset.'

'She'll be left with Glenda,' said Marina, as they walked down to the hallway

Flame's face darkened. 'Yes,' she said, thoughtfully. 'Listen – there is something I need to tell you about tonight.'

'Can't you tell me now?' asked Marina.

'No, I'd rather tell you when we're ready for bed and not going to be interrupted,' said Flame. 'Better go down now.'

And they ran downstairs to find out more from Mum.

CHAPTER THREE

THE
MOVING PLAN

AT THE supper table that Wednesday evening, there was much discussion about the Glass family. Since Dad had done some architectural work earlier that year for his distant Sprite cousin, Stephen Glass, the two families had got much closer. Recently, Verena had told her father how unhappy she was living at The Oaks with her grandmother. He had asked Colin and Ottalie to keep on eye on his daughter, as his work often took him away from home. As a result, Mum and Dad felt a sense of responsibility towards Verena.

When they recently heard the news that Zoe – Verena's mother – not only wanted to come home, but her father Stephen wanted her to, everyone in the Sprite family had been delighted. So there was a great sense of disappointment about the delay. Mum, particularly, was conscious of the effect on Verena.

'Poor girl!' said Mum, for the umpteenth time. 'It's such a shame – just before Christmas and as everything between her parents was looking so positive.'

'Zoe's still coming back, Ottalie,' Dad reminded her. 'It'll just be a few days later than it would have been.'

'I know, I know,' said Mum. 'But it's just such a shame – and I expect Verena is very upset.'

'Yes, she is,' said Marina. 'She called me.'

'She called you?' said Flame, with a quizzical look.

'Yes,' replied Marina, with a face that said, 'And why shouldn't she?' Marina and Verena had been friends for some months.

'It's just that . . .' Flame's voice faded off. It was not the time to talk about her feelings about Verena right now, in front of Mum and Dad.

Marina shot her elder sister a look, but Flame was staring at the table.

When the meal finished and they were clearing the table, Marina asked Flame quietly, 'What was that about? You looked worried. Is it something to do with Verena?'

Flame looked into Marina's kind blue eyes and nodded. 'I'm not sure, but I think so.'

That night, as soon as Mum had said goodnight and gone downstairs, Marina, Ash and Ariel crept along the corridor to Flame's bedroom in their dressing gowns and huddled on her bright red duvet.

'It's so cold,' shivered Ariel, getting under the duvet. 'Can't you warm up the room a bit, Flame?'

Flame was crouched down on the carpet by her bookshelf, getting out the small wooden box.

'Yes, come on,' added Ash, with a smile. 'Warm it up a bit in here before we all freeze!'

'You're not serious?' said Flame, standing up.

'Yes, we are!' laughed Marina. 'It's cold in here! Use your magic!'

Flame shook her head in disbelief. 'Honestly,' she muttered with a smile, putting down the box. 'I'm not sure this is a proper use of my power.'

'Stop being such a prissy, Flame!' laughed Marina. 'It's a good idea.'

For a few seconds, Flame stood in the middle of the room, thinking. 'It *is* pretty chilly in here,' she agreed. 'Okay then.'

Marina, Ash and Ariel watched as Flame held out her long arms straight and raised them slightly above the level of her head. She pointed her index fingers and closed her eyes, then turned slowly in a circle.

In her mind, Flame Sprite summoned her magic power of Fire. As she turned in a circle on the carpet, a gentle blue light began to glow around her hands and the air began to warm up.

'Oooh, that's better!' giggled Ariel.

A minute later, when the room was warm as toast, Flame picked up the wooden box and sat down on her bed beside her sisters.

'I hope Mum doesn't walk in,' said Ash, with a smile. 'You'll have some explaining to do if she feels the heat in this room!'

Flame smiled as she opened the box. 'We should be safe for now – I think she and Dad are sitting by the fire, reading.'

'So what's happened?' asked Marina. 'What is it you want to show us?'

Flame took the plan out of the box, opened it and laid it on the duvet. 'Do you remember George told us to watch the plan closely, as it would change?'

'Yes,' her sisters replied, crowding round.

'Well, look here,' said Flame. 'I think there's a new mark. I wonder if you can spot it?'

Her sisters peered at the marks and squiggles, then shook their heads.

Flame pointed to the small black mark in the centre of the West Tower. 'Look there,' she said.

Ariel frowned, then looked up at Flame. 'It's a black dot.'

'Yes, but it wasn't there before,' said Flame.

'How do you know?' asked Ariel.

'Because I look at the secret plan a lot – and I remember what it looks like,' replied Flame. 'This is a new mark.'

'What does it *mean*?' asked Ash.

'I think it means that something is changing in the magic at Sprite Towers,' said Flame.

'Fab fantastic!' said Ariel. 'More magic!'

'Mrs Duggery told us there was treasure to be found at Sprite Towers,' Marina reminded her.

'Yes, she did,' said Ash. She reached into her dressing-gown pocket. 'Hang on a mo – my magic stone is vibrating.'

Flame, Marina and Ariel watched as Ash held up the magic stone on the open palm of her hand. A faint blue light began to pulse through the stone.

'It's so pretty,' said Ariel. 'I love the colour of the blue light.'

'It's the same colour as the light that comes when we make the Circle of Power,' said Marina.

'It vibrated just as Marina said whatever it was about Mrs Duggery and the treasure,' said Ash, staring at the stone.

Flame gazed at the stone, then looked up at her sisters and said, 'There's something else I need to tell you.'

As Ash put the magic stone back in her pocket, Flame told her sisters about the feeling that rippled up her arm, how Verena's face kept flashing into her mind – and the missed call from her.

'Now I understand why you thought she'd ring *you*,' murmured Marina.

'Hm,' agreed Flame.

'She didn't say anything to me about it,' said Marina. 'She was very upset about her mother and we talked about that. That, and how she'd be left alone with Glenda, now that her father will be away for longer.'

'We'll see Verena at the church carol concert tomorrow evening,' said Ash. 'We can find out then.'

'We've also got a choir rehearsal in the morning,' said Flame. 'She should be at that.'

'I don't like to think of Verena left alone with Glenda,'

said Ash, resting her chin on her hands.

'No,' agreed Flame. 'If she has got her power, Glenda is sure to sense it.'

'Glenda would try to turn her towards dark power,' said Marina, a concerned look on her face.

Ariel frowned. 'What I don't understand is why Verena would get her power *now*,' she said. 'Don't the Sprites who are going to have magic power get it when they're nine, like us? Why would it come when she's thirteen?'

Flame shook her head. 'I've no idea, pumpkin. Maybe she isn't getting her power at all and it's something else.'

Ash screwed up her face. 'Nah, your feelings are always right, Flame. I'll bet Verena has got her power.'

'It's an *amazing* thought,' murmured Marina. Her sisters looked at her quizzically. 'The idea of another Sprite our age having magic power,' she explained. 'It wouldn't be just us.'

'That's true,' they agreed.

'I hope Verena doesn't get dark magic and fight us,' said Ariel. 'It would be like Grandma and Glenda all over again.'

'That would be a shame,' said Flame, looking thoughtful.

They were silent for a while, then Flame said, 'There's another thing that bothers me: how do we find out about Verena's power, without telling her about ours?'

'What, because Grandma said we should never talk about it to anyone?' asked Ash.

Flame nodded. 'Verena asked me to explain about the Sprite magic power at the firework party a few weeks ago, after she'd overheard Charles and Glenda talking.'

'What did you say?' asked Ash.

'That I couldn't say anything, but that she would find out when the time came,' said Flame.

'Maybe you should ask Grandma what she thinks,' suggested Ash.

'Yes,' agreed Flame.

Ariel yawned.

'Let's sleep on it now,' said Flame.

But Verena Glass was not at the rehearsal on Thursday morning. Just as Mum parked the big red car at the village church, she got a call on her mobile.

'That was Stephen Glass,' she said to the girls as she put her phone away. 'He's come home from London to see Verena and Glenda before he flies off to Buenos Aires this evening. He says Verena won't be coming to the rehearsal and that Glenda will bring her to the concert this evening.'

So that was that. 'We'll have to wait,' Flame said to Marina, as they got out of the car.

'Seems so,' agreed Marina.

For the next hour and a half, Mum and her four daughters rehearsed carols for the concert with other members of the Christmas choir. As the star singer Verena was missed, but everyone understood why.

The rest of the day passed busily but peacefully, though Flame felt an underlying sense of anxiety. Something's going to happen, she thought. I just know it. When she checked the plan in the afternoon, sure enough, the little black dot in the middle of the West Tower had grown a fraction larger.

Flame gasped. I *knew* it, she thought.

* * *

It was a clear, cold evening as the Sprite family walked up the path to the church at six o'clock. The Sprite Sisters looked out for Verena among the crowd of people. As soon as she saw them, she came up and first said hello to Mum and Dad.

The Sprite Sisters glanced at one another – they knew something was up. Verena's face had a look of excitement and tension they had never seen before. As their parents expressed sorrow at her mother's accident, Verena smiled gratefully. As soon as she could, she moved away and grabbed Flame's arm. 'I must speak with you!' she whispered.

Flame nodded and the two girls moved to the side. Marina, Ash and Ariel looked at one another. 'We'll find out soon enough,' said Ash.

'Glenda's here,' said Marina, glancing towards the pews at the front of the nave.

'I hope she doesn't spoil this concert like she did the one at school,' whispered Ariel.

'No, I'm sure she won't – not tonight,' said Ash.

'I don't trust that woman one bit,' whispered Ariel.

'None of us do,' whispered Marina. 'Let's get to our places. We'll be starting in a few minutes.'

There was little time to talk, but as quietly and as quickly as she could, Verena told Flame about lighting up the bulb with her finger.

Flame's mouth dropped open in surprise. 'Oh my goodness,' she whispered, staring at Verena's face.

'I had to tell you,' said Verena. 'I thought I was going

mad! You do believe me, don't you?'

Flame registered the anxiety in the girl's eyes. What do I say, she thought. If I reply 'yes', Verena will know I know about magic powers. If I say 'no', that would be a lie. Here is the girl who has been my hated rival, now begging me for help.

Flame smiled, but said nothing.

Verena took this as an affirmation and exhaled in a burst. Relief flooded over her face. 'I wish I understood what is happening to me,' she said. 'I really need to talk to you about it properly. Can I come over and see you tomorrow? I'm really worried about what my grandmother is going to do. I'm sure she knows something has happened to me. She's watching me like a hawk.'

Flame looked at Verena, still unsure how to react.

'Please – I really need to talk to you,' repeated Verena.

'I should think it will be okay – I'll ask Mum afterwards,' said Flame. She glanced around, aware suddenly that people were settling. 'We'd better get to our places. I think they're ready to start.'

As Flame moved to her row, beside Marina, her sister whispered, 'What did Verena say?'

Flame whispered into her ear, 'That she could light up a light bulb with her finger.'

Marina's mouth dropped open, as she stared round at Flame with wide eyes.

Beside her, Ash tugged her sleeve. Marina whispered the news to her.

Ash blinked in astonishment. 'Blimey,' she gasped under

her breath, then turned to whisper to the youngest Sprite.

Ariel's grey eyes grew as big as saucers. She stared ahead, her mouth open wide.

Worried Ariel might say something out loud, Ash put her finger up over her mouth, to indicate 'Shh'.

The four girls all leaned round to exchange glances of amazement, then looked at Verena standing in front of them.

Thirty seconds later, the concert began. Reverend Hodges, the vicar, introduced the choir and thanked the choir-master, Mr Watkins. The audience clapped, then stood to sing the first carol, 'Once in Royal David's City'. Suddenly, the ancient church was filled with music; bathed in the glow of candlelight, everything felt peaceful and warm.

The audience sat down for the second carol, which was to be sung by the choir. As the lead soprano, Verena stood out at the front. Mr Watkins raised his baton and looked at Verena, who led the way. Her voice shone out. Behind her stood the four Sprite Sisters. Mum stood with the altos, at the other side.

As the Sprite Sisters sang out loud and clear, they registered the smiles of the audience. Dad and Grandma sat in a pew on the south side of the nave, beaming happily. Only one person sat stony-faced: when the girls caught her glance, Glenda Glass's cold blue eyes seemed to bore a hole through them. But each of the sisters was also aware that Glenda was not *really* watching them: this evening, her attention was focused on Verena.

I'm not surprised, thought Flame. I wonder if Glenda is pleased or threatened by the idea that her granddaughter has the magic power of the Sprite family?

Flame shivered suddenly – registered a feeling of fear passing through her body. Verena will be alone with Glenda at The Oaks, she thought. She will be totally exposed to Glenda's dark power – and her influence.

Her feeling of fear increased when the concert finished and Verena came up to her, white-faced.

'Grandma says I can't come round tomorrow,' she said. 'She says we've got to decorate the Christmas tree. Can I call you?'

'Yes,' said Flame, seeing Glenda waiting for Verena, just behind her.

Verena squeezed her arm quickly. 'Thank you,' she said, then moved away.

'Well done!' people said to Verena, as she followed Glenda towards the church door.

'Mrs Glass, aren't you and Verena stopping to have coffee with us?' Reverend Hodges asked, as they passed.

Glenda turned to him. 'Thank you, Reverend, but no. We have to get home.'

'Your granddaughter sings like an angel,' said Reverend Hodges, smiling at Verena. 'You should be very proud of her.'

Glenda's cold blue eyes flashed. 'I *am*,' she said.

Reverend Hodges gave her a weak smile, then thanked Verena warmly for all her effort.

As they reached the door, Mum came towards Verena and

gave her a big hug. 'Well done, Verena – you sang beautifully!' she enthused. 'You really have a gift.'

Verena smiled happily. 'Do you think so? I'd love to be a singer when I'm grown up.'

'Yes, yes!' laughed Mum. 'I've always thought so.' She looked over Verena's shoulder at Glenda. 'Hello, Glenda,' she said, politely.

Glenda gave a thin smile. 'Hello, Ottalie,' she said.

'Did Stephen's plane take off on time?' asked Mum.

'Yes, all on time,' said Glenda.

'Well, I hope he finds Zoe in good spirits,' said Mum. 'We are all looking forward to her safe return.'

Verena stepped forward slightly. Mum noticed the look of anxiety on her face as she said, 'Could I come over and see you all soon?'

Mum smiled. 'Of course, dear – you are always welcome.' Then she added, 'Come on Saturday.'

Verena looked round at her grandmother for confirmation. Glenda nodded and said, 'Yes, that's okay.'

At this, Verena's face relaxed into a smile.

'See you then,' smiled Mum. She watched as Verena followed Glenda out of the church. What is wrong with that woman, she wondered. We've had a wonderful evening. It's relaxed and happy here – yet she drags that poor child back to that house the moment it's finished. I hope things improve for Verena when her mother gets home.

On the other side of the church, the Sprite Sisters got fruit drinks and biscuits.

'Did you get a chance to ask Verena anything else?' Ash asked Flame.

'No, Glenda dragged her off the moment the concert finished,' said Flame.

'I saw her speaking to Mum by the door,' said Marina.

'I can't *believe* Verena has a magic power like us,' said Ariel.

'Shh, Ariel!' said her three sisters, looking round. Thankfully no one seemed to have heard.

'I wonder if she's got one of those elly-thingies – you know like we have?' continued Ariel.

'Elements, you mean?' whispered Ash.

'Yes, those,' said Ariel, through a mouthful of juice.

Ash screwed up her mouth. 'Dunno. We'll have to wait and see.'

'You look worried, Flame,' said Marina, looking at her elder sister.

'I *am*,' she agreed. 'I'm worried what Glenda will do – what influence she will have on Verena. She's all alone there now and she doesn't have anyone to talk to.'

'Do you think she's in any danger?' asked Ash.

Flame looked at her sister's soft brown eyes. 'I hope not,' she replied, quietly.

'Anyone close to Glenda Glass is in danger,' said Marina, looking glum.

At that moment, Dad came up to them with a great whoop.

'Splendid!' he said, waving his arms and giving a wide smile. 'Well done, all of you!'

'Thanks Dad!' they all laughed.

'It's a wonderful start to Christmas,' said Dad, smiling at his daughters with pride.

CHAPTER FOUR

VERENA ALONE

THE OAKS felt bigger and lonelier than ever as Verena walked into the house that evening.

She thought of her father, on his way to Buenos Aires. She thought of her mother, lying in hospital seven thousand miles away. She thought of the Sprite family all enjoying themselves in the church hall.

Verena looked round the hallway, as Glenda bolted the door for the night. I feel trapped, she thought. There is no escape from my grandmother now.

'Would you like a mug of hot chocolate?' asked Glenda, walking through to the kitchen and switching on the lights.

'Yes, please,' replied Verena, following her.

'You sang very well this evening,' said Glenda, as she took

milk out of the fridge and poured some into a small saucepan. 'It's a shame your father wasn't here.'

'And Mummy,' added Verena, leaning against one of the kitchen cabinets.

'Yes – and your mother,' said Glenda, putting the milk pan on the hotplate.

Verena stared at the stone floor. Everything around her was expensive and impressive: the kitchen, the clothes she was wearing, the car they had driven back in. But there's an emptiness about it all, she thought. I'd swap all this for a warm and loving family.

'Are you all right, Verena?' asked her grandmother. 'You've seemed very anxious the last two days. Is something the matter? Why do you keep looking at your hands?'

'I'm not!' said Verena, quickly, putting her hands down by her side.

Glenda gave a thin smile. 'Are they feeling different?'

'My hands? No – no, they're . . . they're just the same as always,' said Verena.

'I wondered if they were tingling,' said Glenda, as she poured hot milk into a mug and stirred it.

'Tingling?' asked Verena, with a gasp of surprise. What do I say, she thought. She mustn't know, she mustn't know what is happening to me . . .

'Yes,' said Glenda, handing her the mug of hot chocolate and looking her straight in the eye. '*Tingling.*'

Verena stared at her grandmother and blinked.

Glenda held her gaze for a few seconds, then turned and moved away. 'I had the feeling your hands may be tingling,' she said, switching on the kettle.

Verena stood still as a statue, holding her mug in front of her.

'It's just that, when I was about your age, my hands started to tingle,' said Glenda, turning to look at Verena. 'And it made me feel very anxious, as I did not know why.'

Glenda waited, watching her granddaughter, but Verena was silent, staring at her mug. After a few seconds, Glenda said, 'I should go up to bed now. You've had a long day. Tomorrow we'll decorate the Christmas tree.'

'Yes,' said Verena, quickly. 'Yes – I'll go up now. Night, Grandma – and thank you for the hot chocolate.' As fast as she could without spilling her drink, she ran up the staircase to her room.

Once inside, she gasped. She stood against the door, looking into the dark. Then she put down the mug on the floor, touched the doorknob with her left hand and pointed her right index finger at the cerise light on the ceiling.

She felt a whoosh of power through her right arm and – *bing!* – the light came on. As it did, the switch clicked down on the wall on its own. Verena stared at it for a few seconds, then picked up her mug from the floor and put it on the bedside table.

I'm frightened what this magic power means, she thought, sitting down heavily on the edge of her bed. Am I some sort of freak? What will happen to me? Will people know I am different?

It's getting stronger: I can feel it, she thought, lying down on the bed. I don't know what to do. I'm so confused – and

I feel so alone. Grandma's watching me all the time. I'm sure she can see I've changed. Oh, I wish Mummy would come home soon . . .

Verena turned her face into the pillow and sobbed and sobbed.

Half an hour later, her grandmother knocked on her door and opened it. She saw Verena lying curled up, still dressed, on her bed.

'Verena, why aren't you in bed?' she asked. 'It's cold – get undressed and get into bed properly.'

Verena sat up slowly and stared at the floor. The mug of hot chocolate sat cold and half drunk on her bedside table.

Standing in the doorway, Glenda looked at her grand-daughter's sad face, noticed the streaks of tears on her cheeks.

Glenda Glass's heart had been dead for so long that seeing her granddaughter like this did not upset her. She simply said, 'Get into bed and get warm, Verena – and go to sleep now.'

Verena nodded, staring at the floor.

'Goodnight,' said Glenda, as she closed the door.

Verena dragged herself off the bed and changed into her pyjamas. Then she walked to the switch by the door and turned out the light, walked back across the carpet in the dark and climbed into bed. Shivering, she gathered the duvet around her and wondered what the morning would bring. Then she cried some more.

Downstairs in the drawing room, Glenda Glass sat down on the cream silk sofa and stared ahead. Apart from the light from the table lamp beside her, the room was dark.

I'm *sure* Verena has found her power, she thought. I can sense it. There's something about her that is different – and she's been so secretive the last few days. Is that what her tears were about, or is she just upset about her mother?

I was about her age when I got my power, and so was my mother, Glenda remembered. If Verena was going to inherit the magic that runs thorough the Sprite family, it would probably follow the same path as ours.

The Sprite Sisters seem to have been much younger when they got their power, she thought. There is no rule-book when it comes to magic power.

But, at the thought of the Sprite Sisters, the expression hardened on Glenda's face. With her right hand, she smoothed back her pale blond hair, which was pulled into a chignon on the nape of her neck. It was the only soft part of her. Every other feature was sharp: her thin nose and cruel mouth, her cold blue eyes and imperious expression.

My magic power has meant I've got a lot of things that I may not otherwise have been able to have, she thought. The Sprite branch of the family might choose to use their magic kindly and wisely, but I have used mine to get what I want: money, property, status – power over people.

With Marilyn Sprite's money in the bank, I'm a very wealthy lady, she thought. Wealthy enough without it – but even more wealthy with it, she thought with a smile.

And now it seems Verena has got her power. What use can I put it to? How can it benefit me?

When Zoe left six months earlier, Stephen had invited his mother to come to live at The Oaks and look after Verena, since he was away working in London most of the time. Neither Stephen nor Zoe had realised that Glenda had used her dark power to spoil their marriage and deliberately create the situation that would open the way to living here. And being *here* meant she was close to Sprite Towers.

Glenda's lips tightened into a line. It had been a challenging six months battling the Sprite Sisters.

And apart from that, she considered, there was the worrying question of Marilyn Sprite's stolen money. Glenda had thought she had hidden it well, but was beginning to feel uncomfortable. Marilyn had been to the south of France asking questions, she had learned. Verena mentioned she had spoken to the police there. Perhaps it is not well hidden enough, she wondered.

Nothing has gone the way I planned it, she thought. It's almost Christmas and I'm no closer to getting Sprite Towers or having the secret plan that leads to the magic at the heart of the house. At every turn, the Sprite Sisters have outwitted me – them and Mrs Duggery.

Glenda smiled a grim smile.

Now Verena has her power, *I* shall have an ally, she thought. It's time we had more dark power in the family. Verena is young and open to influence. She's confused, judging by this evening's tears.

Let's see what pressure I can apply tomorrow, she thought, getting up and switching off the light. I shall find a way to make sure Verena uses her power against the Sprite Sisters – and get hold of that house and plan at last. Then, perhaps, I shall be in a stronger position to keep the money.

CHAPTER FIVE

DARK
MAGIC

ALL DAY Friday, Flame Sprite waited for Verena's call.

'What do you think is happening over there?' she asked Marina, late that afternoon. 'Verena said she'd call me and I haven't heard from her. It's making me nervous. I wish we could do something.'

'She must be terrified, locked in that house with Glenda Glass,' said Marina, her face troubled.

'All we can do now is wait until tomorrow,' said Ash.

'That's if Glenda still allows her over here,' said Flame, with a frown.

'There must be something we can do to help her,' said Marina. They were silent for a few seconds, each thinking on this.

Then Ariel piped up. 'How about we make the Circle of Power and send Verena some magic light to make her feel better?'

Flame, Marina and Ash stared at their little sister. Despite her dreamy demeanour and ability to get them all into trouble, the youngest Sprite often came up with exactly the right idea.

'That's a really good idea, Ariel!' said Marina, with a big smile.

'Good thinking,' said Flame. 'Let's go up to the East Tower now. Mum's out for a bit and Dad's at the office in town.'

And they raced up the stairs to the tower.

There the Sprite Sisters stood in a circle and held hands. Flame stood at the east side of the circle and summoned her power of Fire. Marina stood at the south and summoned her power of Water. Ash stood at the west and invoked the power of Earth and Ariel stood at the north, calling on her power of Air.

'East, south, west and north – our powers are balanced,' said Flame. As she said this, a small blue light began to flicker around them, as if moving through their arms and bodies. Second by second, the light grew stronger and stronger until it was a deep, bright blue surging through them and around them.

'The Circle of Power,' said Flame.

The four sisters stood with their eyes closed and enjoyed the peaceful feeling of the blue light. Then Flame said, 'Let's send this light to Verena. Let's picture her in our minds and imagine her sharing this light with us. See her happy and confident – and unafraid of Glenda Glass.'

As the Sprite Sisters thought of Verena Glass, the blue light strengthened even more.

The faces of the four girls were happy and calm, and when the light faded a few minutes later they opened their eyes and laughed.

'That was lovely,' said Ash, with her quiet smile.

'Hm,' agreed Marina, staring up at the high arched windows.

Ariel yawned. 'I feel all relaxed and sleepy. I wonder if Verena feels sleepy too?'

Her sisters laughed.

'Let's hope that it helped her,' said Flame.

At that moment, they heard their mother calling up the stairs. 'Girls – come down for tea, please!'

The four Sprite Sisters looked at one another and laughed. 'Oops!' giggled Ash.

'That was well timed,' said Marina.

'Yes, one of these days Mum will find us using our magic power – and then we'll be for it,' said Flame, opening the wooden door at the side of the tower.

They raced round and round the huge mahogany staircase, all the way down to the hallway at the bottom.

Meanwhile, at The Oaks, Verena had been experiencing one of the most difficult days of her life.

The trouble began at breakfast, when her grandmother asked her if her hands were still tingling. Verena was tempted to say they weren't, but knew Glenda would see through her. There was no hiding from her grandmother: that she already knew.

But at the same time, she thought to herself, I'm not going to let her push me about.

She dug in, answering Glenda's questions slowly, deliberately drawing everything out as long as she could.

Her grandmother's temper was on a short fuse, however. After months of struggling against the Sprite Sisters, she was in no mood to be thwarted by an irksome teenager.

Sensing the potential full force of Glenda's temper, Verena decided it was safer to sit still and listen. At which point, Glenda dived straight in.

'You've inherited the magic power that runs through the Sprite family,' she announced, fixing Verena with her cold blue eyes. 'But you already know that.'

'I don't,' replied Verena. 'I don't know what's happening.'

'Well, perhaps you would begin by explaining to me what you are feeling – and what happens if you point that finger of yours.'

Verena looked down at her right index finger.

'Well?' said Glenda. 'Come on – I haven't got all day.'

Verena exhaled, then said in a quiet voice, 'I can light up the light without touching the switch.'

'Ah,' said Glenda, with a satisfied smile. 'Well, that's very helpful.'

'Why?' asked Verena.

Glenda laughed a short, hard laugh. 'It's helpful to me, Verena.'

'But why?' asked Verena again. 'What do you expect me to do? Save on the electricity bill?'

'Don't be childish,' said Glenda, with the hint of a snarl.

Verena sank down into her chair.

'There are ways of using your magic power,' said Glenda, smoothing down her hair.

'Good way and bad ways?' asked Verena.

Glenda nodded. 'Something like that.'

Then Glenda started talking. She talked and talked. She talked about the Sprites and how they had thwarted her. She talked about the magic in their house. She told Verena about the suffering of her grandmother, Margaret, who had come back to haunt Sprite Towers.

To all this, Verena listened with one ear. But, as her grandmother talked, part of her began to wonder whether to confront her about the conversation with Charles Smythson. Since she had overheard that argument at the end of October, Verena had always wondered if Glenda had been aware that she was listening.

I wonder what she would do if she knew *I knew* she had stolen Marilyn's money, she thought. If my grandmother doesn't know I know about the extent of her scheming, maybe I can use this to *my* advantage . . .

And she sat up slightly in her chair.

Glenda took this movement as a sign of interest in what she was saying. 'So you see, Verena, we have work to do, you and I. Don't you agree?'

Verena blinked. 'Perhaps,' she answered, cautiously.

'Perhaps?' said Glenda. 'Don't you want to own Sprite

Towers and own the secret power of the family's magic?'

Verena hesitated. Caution is the best way, she thought. 'Grandma, this is an awful lot for me to take on board right now,' she said. 'I'm worried about Mummy. I suddenly find I can turn on lights by pointing my finger at them. Now you're telling me about secret power. My head is a whirl.'

Glenda looked at Verena suspiciously.

'Please, Grandma! Can we just do one thing at a time?'

'What would you suggest we do first?' asked Glenda.

'Can you explain how I control this power, please?'

Glenda inhaled, impatiently. The girl's question seemed reasonable enough, though. Maybe it would help to explain things.

'Who explained to you about your power – and when did you get it?' asked Verena quickly.

'When I was around your age,' replied Glenda. 'My mother explained it to me.'

'My mother is not a Sprite,' said Verena.

'And your father does not have the magic power that runs through part of the Sprite family,' said Glenda. 'Not many men do. So it seems you will have to rely on me to explain.'

'What do you use your power for?' asked Verena.

Glenda laughed another hard laugh. 'To get what I want.'

'Is that what it's meant for?' Verena tensed as Glenda looked at her with cold eyes. 'I mean – couldn't you use your power to help people?' she said, quickly.

'Some would say so,' replied Glenda, looking down at her hands.

'What's the best thing you've done with your power?'

'Hm . . .' Glenda replied slowly – and then was silent.

'Where does the power come from, Grandma?' asked Verena.

Glenda shook her head. 'Who knows? It's just *there*. Very few people have it. Most people would say it's all bunk.'

'Does your power come through your hands?'

'Yes,' replied Glenda, holding out her long, thin hands. 'It comes through my fingers.'

'And you point your finger at things?' asked Verena, who had wanted to use the word 'people', but decided against it.

'Yes,' agreed Glenda.

'Can you show me?'

Glenda considered this for a moment. Then she got up and walked towards the kitchen window. On the bird table outside, a robin was pecking at some seeds.

Glenda focused her eyes on the robin and lifted her finger. Before Verena could say, '*No!*' a flash of power shot out of her hands. The small bird keeled over – and lay with its legs in the air.

Verena cried out. '*Oh Grandma – you've killed it!*'

'Yes,' agreed Glenda.

'But that's a *dreadful* thing to do!' cried Verena, staring at her in horror.

'It's a lesson to you,' said Glenda, turning to her. 'Now

you know what I can – and will – do, and why. If I ask you to do something, you will please do it.'

Verena looked at the little bird and stood, transfixed. 'I didn't mean you to hurt anything, Grandma,' she said, quietly. A large teardrop rolled down her cheek.

Then she moved towards the kitchen door. 'I'm going out to bury the robin,' she said.

'As you wish,' said Glenda.

Verena opened the door, then turned and looked back at Glenda, her blue eyes wide and clear. In a quiet voice she said, 'You know, Grandma, when you came here to look after me in June, I was so pleased. I thought you'd love me and we'd be friends and have fun together. I'm sorry that hasn't happened. If *this* is what having magic power means, then I don't want it.'

For a second, she looked into her grandmother's eyes.

Her words hung in the air as she turned and went out of the door.

Glenda turned and watched through the window, as Verena lifted the robin off the bird table and carried it down the garden.

The ground was frosty and it took some time for Verena to dig the hole to bury the robin. Tears rolled down her cheeks as she stabbed at the hard earth with the spade.

Grandma's mad, she thought. She's mad and bad – and *horrible*. How could she *do* that to that poor little bird – just to show me her power!

I've got to talk to Flame and her sisters, she thought, as

she smoothed the soil down on the top of the hole. I'll call her now.

No, it's too dangerous. Grandma might hear me. Then I'll be for it. But will she let me go there tomorrow?

Well, if she doesn't I'll creep out and cycle over – or walk. I've *got* to see the Sprites!

When she came back into the house, her grandmother seemed subdued.

'We were going to do the tree today, Verena,' said Glenda. 'Would you like to help?'

'Yes,' replied Verena, noting a slight change in her tone. 'I'll just go and wash my hands.'

A few minutes later, in silence, they strung the fairy lights around the huge tree that stood in the hallway.

For the next hour, they hung beautiful coloured baubles from the top to the bottom of the tree.

It's not like this when I decorate the Christmas tree with Mummy, thought Verena. We laugh and have fun.

But she carried on and worked hard, wanting to make the tree look as pretty as possible for her mother's return. Once or twice, she looked across at her grandmother – who seemed very quiet.

As soon as the tree was finished, Verena went up to her bedroom and shut the door. There she lay down on the bed and closed her eyes.

As the Sprite Sisters beamed over the light from their Circle of Power, Verena fell into a deep and restful sleep, unaware that she was engulfed in a beautiful blue light.

When she woke an hour later, it was pitch dark. As she reached for the lamp switch, somewhere deep in her heart Verena Glass felt a new sense of hope, of brightness and of peace.

At Sprite Towers that evening, Flame talked to her grandmother in the quiet of her sitting room on the first floor of the house. Since Marilyn Sprite came to live with them four years ago, Flame and she had become very close. The two Sprites were similar in shape and colouring: both tall and long-limbed with green eyes and dark copper-coloured hair, though Marilyn's had now faded with age. Their temperaments, too, were alike. Both had quick, analytical minds, liked things to be organised and did not suffer fools.

All the Sprite Sisters regarded their grandmother as their mentor on the subject of magic power. She had been guiding them since they each came into their power at the age of nine.

Flame, however, regarded her grandmother as her mentor on all aspects of life. Often, she came to her grandmother's sitting room and they would sit on the armchairs and talk together.

This evening, Flame had brought the secret plan. She laid it out on the small rosewood table in front of her grandmother and pointed.

'Look, Grandma, the plan has changed again. See that squiggle here – well, that was a dot yesterday. Before that, there was no mark there at all. George Sprite told us to watch the plan, as it would change. I've been studying it regularly, so I know I'm right about this mark.'

'I wonder what it means?' said her grandmother, peering at the black squiggle.

'I don't know, but I have a real sense that something is about to happen,' said Flame.

'Then I'm sure you'll know what it means when the time comes,' replied Grandma. 'Always trust your feelings.'

For the next few minutes, Flame told her grandmother about Verena.

'And she just told you – just like that? In the middle of the church?' Grandma looked horrified. 'Well, I hope no one overheard!'

'Nobody heard, Grandma – Verena whispered it very quietly to me,' said Flame. 'Aren't you surprised she's found her power?'

Grandma pursed her lips. 'Yes – and no.'

'How do you mean?' asked Flame.

'I remember Mrs Duggery telling me once, many years ago, that Glenda's branch of the family came into their power a bit later than our branch. When I asked why it was different, she said it "just was".'

'Sounds like Mrs Duggery,' laughed Flame.

'Yes,' agreed Grandma, with a smile.

'But what do we do about Verena?' asked Flame. 'When she comes over tomorrow, she'll tell us about her power. Do we tell her about ours? I'm sure she's in danger over there, locked in at The Oaks with Glenda. We went up to the tower and made the Circle of Power this afternoon and sent her that light.'

'That was a nice thing to do, Flame,' said Grandma. 'I'm sure it will help her.'

'Thank you,' said Flame.

Grandma looked across the sitting room and sighed a heavy sigh. 'Things are getting more complicated with Glenda. There's also the question outstanding of what we do about my stolen money. I think I've got enough evidence now to turn Glenda in to the police. She could go to prison and that would make things very difficult within the family. Your father and Stephen Glass do quite a bit of work together – and now Zoe's coming home, it would be nice for things to be settled.'

'But if Glenda's behaved badly, she deserves to be punished!' said Flame. 'And you *need* your money back!'

'I agree with you on both counts, but it's not that simple,' said Grandma, shaking her head. 'Oh dear, what is to be done, I wonder?'

'Could you ask Glenda to give you the money back?' suggested Flame.

'I have wondered about that,' replied her grandmother. 'I'm not sure she'd listen at the moment.'

They were silent for a while, thinking on this. Then Flame said, 'So what shall we say to Verena about our powers tomorrow? Will our magic weaken if we speak about it?'

'Your powers will not weaken if you speak to another Sprite, no,' said Grandma. 'Where you have to be very careful is talking to people who are not Sprites. Your powers would weaken then – and you'd be very exposed. People would not believe you and things could be made difficult for you. But I think your problem is more about Glenda getting knowledge of you through Verena. She's bound to be influencing the girl. She could try to find out things to use against us all.'

'I know – I'm really worried about that,' agreed Flame.

'Glenda will think she has an ally at last – someone she could force to use dark power,' said Grandma.

'She's lost Charles's support, so she'll look to Verena?' asked Flame.

'Yes, something like that.' Grandma was silent for a while, then she said, 'In the light of this, I should let Verena tell you as much as she wants, but you tell her as little as you can – just until you're certain you can trust her.'

'That sounds like good advice, Grandma,' said Flame, and she got up to give her a hug.

'Goodnight, love,' said Grandma. 'Sleep well – and well done for spotting the changing plan.'

'Goodnight, Grandma, and thank you,' said Flame. She picked up the plan from the table and closed the door.

Up in her bedroom, she had one more look at the plan, then put it back in the small wooden box behind her books on the shelf.

Five minutes later, Flame lay in her bed, gazing up at the ceiling. She half expected her sisters to come in, but they were all asleep, tired out by the day's activities.

I wonder how Verena is, she thought. And I wonder how we could get Glenda to return Grandma's money?

I'll think about that tomorrow, she thought, yawning. Then she switched off her bedside light and went to sleep.

CHAPTER SIX

VERENA SHOWS
HER POWER

IT WAS a frosty morning when Glenda dropped off Verena at Sprite Towers on Saturday. She was reluctant to let her granddaughter go to see the Sprite Sisters, but Verena was adamant. The mile drive along the country lane was tense and by the time they arrived, Verena was desperate to get out of the car and away from Glenda.

Mum was struck by how anxious Verena looked as she came into the kitchen with the girls. 'How's your mother?' she asked, after giving her a hug.

'I spoke to her this morning and she's feeling better, thank you,' said Verena.

'That's good news,' said Mum. 'And they're still planning to fly home on Christmas Eve?'

'Yes,' Verena replied. 'I really hope they'll be here.'

'So, how are things at home – with your grandmother?'

Verena shot Mum an uncertain look. 'How do you mean?'

'Well – I just wondered if you were getting on all right,' said Mum, feeling she'd put her foot in it some way, but not sure why. The Sprite family knew that Verena was unhappy living with Glenda – Verena had told Mum so herself, only a few weeks before.

'Er, well, it's not easy,' said Verena, looking down at the floor, her face tense. Mum waited – but Verena was silent. She glanced up at the Sprite Sisters, who all stood waiting with anxious looks on their faces.

Suddenly Mum felt she was treading on eggshells. 'Okay . . . well, I expect you've all got lots to talk about,' she said.

'Yes!' said Verena, with a smile. 'See you later!'

Mum watched as she dashed past and the five girls shot out of the kitchen.

'Verena seems very tense,' Mum commented to Grandma, who was making mince pies on the kitchen table.

'Yes, she did a bit,' agreed Grandma, looking up.

'I wonder what the matter is?'

'I expect she's worried about her mother.'

'Could be, but it felt as if there was something else,' said Mum. 'Something the girls know about. Did you notice the way they were waiting for me to stop talking and how quickly they all shot out of the kitchen?

Grandma smiled. 'It's probably something about a boy.'

Mum laughed. 'Yes, I expect you're right!'

The Sprite Sisters and Verena Glass bounded up the wide mahogany stairs to the second floor and into Flame's bedroom. Ash banged the door shut behind them and they sat down in a circle on the navy carpet.

The Sprite Sisters all looked at Verena.

'So tell us what's been happening,' said Flame. 'We're intrigued about you being able to turn on a light bulb.'

Verena looked at Flame. 'I didn't realise you'd tell your sisters,' she said.

Flame laughed. 'We don't have secrets!'

'We're dying to know about the light bulb!' said Ariel. 'Please tell us!'

Verena smiled. For a few seconds she looked down at the carpet, her long blond hair falling forward, her expression thoughtful. She lifted her beautiful face and smiled at them one by one.

'I'll start at the beginning,' she said. The Sprite Sisters sat silent, listening, as Verena told them about her experience with the ghost of Margaret Sprite at their Hallowe'en party a few weeks before.

'We were playing Sardines and I was up on the attics corridor,' she explained. 'I saw this whirling "thing" come up to me. It was like a grey shadow, but in it I could see a woman's face – and hands reaching out. I thought it might be the ghost – I'd already seen what it could do, remember – and that I'd be scared. But I *wasn't*! It was really strange, but I felt safe – *knew* somehow that it wouldn't harm me.'

Then she looked across at Flame, sitting opposite. 'And Flame was watching me,' she said. 'She saw the ghost spin around me – and that I wasn't scared.'

Marina, Ash and Ariel looked around at Flame. 'You didn't tell us,' they said.

Verena gave Flame a wry smile. 'It seems you have some secrets after all.'

'Why didn't you say anything, Flame?' asked Marina.

Flame shrugged. 'I didn't keep it deliberately secret. I was thinking about what it meant – then I forgot about it.'

'And there was another thing about the ghost,' said Verena, eager to carry on. 'I heard it say the words "magic power".'

Marina, Ash and Ariel looked at Verena, then each other.

'You heard the ghost *speak*?' asked Ariel.

Verena nodded.

'Golly,' said Ariel.

'Did you hear the ghost speak, Flame?' asked Marina.

Flame shook her head. 'No, but I knew something had happened – and I felt a sense of connection to Verena, in a way I hadn't before.'

'So did I with you,' said Verena, looking across at Flame. 'Then, a few days later, I spoke to you at the fireworks party – you remember?'

'And you told me you'd overheard Charles Smythson arguing with your grandmother and you wanted to know what "magic power" meant,' replied Flame.

'But you wouldn't tell me,' said Verena. 'You said I would understand when the time came.'

Flame caught Verena's glance. For a few seconds the two girls held each other's gaze.

'There are some things you don't talk about,' said Flame. 'It wasn't a matter of choice.' She was silent for a moment, then added, 'I had a sense that the time would come when this may change.'

Verena nodded, then said in a quiet voice, 'Since I overheard Charles and Grandma's argument, I thought a lot about what he meant when he talked about "magic power" in the Sprite family – but I didn't understand. I knew my grandmother was a difficult and cold woman, but he accused her of some *awful* things – like hurting you sisters and stealing your grandmother's money.' Verena looked round at the Sprite Sisters. 'Your faces suggest to me that you already know this,' she said.

Marina and Ash looked at Flame. They wondered what she would say in response to this, but Ariel butted in.

Pushing her ski-jump nose in the air, she squeaked, 'Tell us what's happened *now*! I want to know about the light bulb!'

Verena looked round at her and laughed. 'Okay, okay!'

'Yes, we can come back to that in a minute,' agreed Flame. 'Let's hear what's happened now.'

All eyes were on Verena as she stretched out her right hand and looked at it as she spoke. 'Well, it was all so strange. Three days ago, I felt this tingling sensation through my hands and arms. The feeling built up and up. It was like a strong pulse going down my arm and through my fingers. I didn't know what it meant – thought I might have something wrong with me.'

The Sprite Sisters waited, alert and attentive, as Verena turned her fingers and looked at them. Ariel's eyes were wide with anticipation.

'That Wednesday afternoon I began to feel really confused,' continued Verena. 'The feeling in my arms and hands grew stronger and stronger. At one point, I was feeling tired and lay back on my bed. I think I had my left hand on the iron bedstead behind me. Then I sort of held up my right hand and pointed my finger – like this.'

'Then what did you do?' asked Ariel, her eyes getting bigger and bigger.

Verena considered this for a few seconds. 'Well, I wondered if anything would happen if I sent the "pulse" feeling out through my finger towards the light bulb.'

'And did it?'

Verena laughed. 'Yes – the light came on!'

The Sprite Sisters laughed.

'I was *so* surprised!' said Verena.

'I'll bet you were!' smiled Flame.

'Can you show us?' asked Ariel. 'Show us how you do it!'

Verena laughed awkwardly. 'Well, I'm not sure . . .' The enthusiasm with which she had bounded the stairs to tell the Sprites seemed to have faded. 'I'll feel so silly . . .' she said, her face colouring.

'No, don't,' said Marina, touching her arm gently. 'Just have a go. If it doesn't work, it won't matter.'

'Do you feel your hand tingling now?' asked Ash.

Verena looked into her kind brown eyes. 'Yes – it's there all the time.'

'We'd really appreciate it if you would show us,' said Ash. 'It matters a lot to us.'

'Does it?' asked Verena.

Ash nodded. 'An awful lot.'

Verena sighed and was silent. 'Okay then,' she said, after a few seconds.

She stood up and walked towards the door. The Sprite Sisters moved to the side of the room and sat down in a row on the edge of Flame's bed.

Verena took hold of the brass door handle with her left hand and raised her right hand in the air. She looked at the light bulb with intense concentration – then shook her head and lowered her hand. 'I feel so silly,' she said, quietly.

'You're doing fine,' said Marina.

'It'll be okay – really,' said Flame.

Verena looked up at the light again and raised her right hand. She pointed her index finger at the light bulb and curled her other fingers into her palm.

Her eyes focused on the light bulb. Then, *Whoosh!* – her magic power shot along her arm and out of her finger. *Bing!* The light bulb came on. At the same time, the switch on the wall clicked down.

The Sprite Sisters stared at the light, then at Verena.

'Fantabbydandosish!' said Ariel.

'What?' said Flame, looking round at her. Then she laughed. 'Where on earth do you get your funny words, Ariel?'

'My head,' giggled Ariel.

'Good word, Ariel,' said Verena, standing near the door.

'Well it *was* fantabby-wotsit,' giggled Ariel again. 'I was very impressed!'

'Yes, that was amazing,' said Marina, smiling at Verena. 'Thank you.'

'Can you turn it off?' asked Ash.

Verena paused, then held her finger in the air. Once more the magic power surged through her arm. *Bing!* The light bulb went out and the switch clicked up on the wall.

Flame leaned forward on the bed. 'Do you think you could turn on the bulb without holding the door handle?'

Verena screwed up her face. 'I'll have a go,' she said and held up her finger. This time the light bulb came on for a millisecond, then sputtered out.

Flame stood up and walked towards Verena. She looked down at the door handle, deep in thought. 'Seems there's a connection between your magic power and metal.'

Verena looked at her and waited. Then Flame said, with a look of deep concentration. 'The Chinese regard metal as an element – like fire, water, air and earth.'

Marina, Ash and Ariel exchanged glances, then looked at Flame.

'So you think Verena might work with the element of metal?' asked Marina.

Flame nodded, thoughtfully. 'Hm, could be. Like a conductor – you know, how metal conducts electricity and heat.'

'That's amazing,' said Marina.

Verena moved to the middle of the carpet and sat down. Marina, Ash and Ariel got down off the bed and moved back to the circle. Flame was still staring at the door handle.

'Are you coming to sit down, Flame?' asked Verena.

'Yep,' said Flame and went towards them. As she folded her long legs under her, Verena said, 'I've shared this with you. Now, what I'd like to know – please – is how you all understand what's happening to me. You must know about magic power, otherwise you'd have all been freaked out by what I just showed you – and you weren't. You all sat there cool as cucumbers. Also, I'm sure from what Charles said that you have magic powers. I believe this may be why my grandmother tried to hurt you. So will you please tell me what is going on?'

The Sprite Sisters looked from Verena to each other. Then everybody looked at Flame.

'Do you think your grandmother suspects something is up?' asked Flame, still unsure how to respond to Verena's request.

'Yes, as soon as the tingling feeling started in my arms, I could feel her watching me like a hawk,' said Verena. 'She kept asking me if I was all right.'

'She could sense it,' said Flame.

'So then what happened?' asked Marina.

'Well, Daddy came back on Thursday and we were talking about Mum a lot, so I put the tingling feeling to the back of my mind,' replied Verena. 'Later, at the carol concert, I told Flame about the light bulb, as you all know. And yesterday . . .' Verena's words trailed off and her face looked sad suddenly. She shuddered. 'That was *horrible* . . .'

'What?' the Sprite Sisters all asked. 'What happened?'

Verena stared down at her hands and gave a heavy sigh. The Sprite Sisters exchanged anxious glances. Finally, Verena said, 'My grandmother killed a robin.'

'*What?*' they asked. 'But why?'

Verena sighed again. 'I think she wanted me to see how powerful her magic was – and that she would use it.'

'Blimey,' said Flame, under her breath.

'She's a wicked old lady,' said Ariel, making a cross face.

'How did she do it?' asked Marina.

Verena explained what Glenda had done.

'What an awful thing to do to a bird,' said Ash. 'A Christmas robin.'

Verena caught her gaze. 'Hm,' she agreed. 'Not exactly the spirit of Christmas.'

For a while, the five girls sat with glum faces.

Then Verena said, 'Grandma frightens me.'

Flame looked up. 'I'm not surprised,' she said. She stared down at the floor in silence for a while. Can we tell Verena? she wondered. Can we trust her? She wants to know – and she's shared her secret with us. And we are all Sprites . . .

Flame sighed. But Verena *is* still Glenda Glass's grand-daughter . . .

She looked up and around at each of her sisters, trying to read the expression on their faces. They were each looking at her, waiting, knowing what was going through her mind.

'Tell her, Flame,' said Ash, in her quiet voice.

Marina nodded. 'Yes, tell her.'

Ariel nodded too.

Flame took in a deep breath and murmured, 'Okay.' She drew herself up and sat with her back straight, her eyes focused on Verena.

'Verena, there's something we want to tell you,' she said.

CHAPTER SEVEN

GLENDA CONFRONTED

GLENDA GLASS stared out towards the trees as the last rays of winter sun shone across the wide lawn. She had been staring out of the window a lot. That and pacing about with a restless energy, up and down around the big house.

Why ever did I kill that bird, she wondered for the umpteenth time. What was I thinking? It was bound to upset Verena . . .

For the first time in her life, Glenda felt frightened. This knot of fear in her stomach – she'd never had that before. Not like this. Yes, she'd felt fear when she'd been in a fight, using her magic. But that was different. That was frightening, but exciting. This feeling – it was empty and grey. And it was lonely.

I'm an old woman now, she thought. I'm old and I'm alone. As the sun sank behind the trees, she shivered, crossed her hands over her chest and rubbed her hands up and down her arms. The dark room felt cold, suddenly. She turned to switch on a lamp and looked around.

The house feels empty, she thought. Verena has been away since mid-morning at Sprite Towers. The phone has been silent all day. I'm alone. Rich and powerful, yes – but alone.

Being alone had never worried Glenda Glass before. It meant she could do what she liked, when she liked. She'd had four wealthy husbands, all of them now dead. Each had left her money and she had travelled the world. When her son Stephen was born, she left him in the care of a nanny and hardly ever saw him. If anyone had tried to thwart her plans, she had used her magic power against them – even her husbands, though they did not know it. She'd hidden her power successfully all these years.

Nobody ever tried to thwart me twice, she thought, with a cold smile. Well – not until the Sprite Sisters. And that Duggery woman . . .

Glenda's expression hardened as she stared across the room. The Sprite Sisters and Mrs Duggery have all been a damn nuisance, she thought, her mouth curling at one side.

Since she'd come to The Oaks in June, she had tried to get rid of the Sprite Sisters. She had tried to get hold of Sprite Towers. And she'd tried to get hold of the secret plan that she knew the girls had got. And nothing had worked.

Each time, the girls or Mrs Duggery have knocked me back, she thought, her eyes narrowing.

So has it been worth it, she wondered. What have I *really* achieved?

She held this thought for a moment, but it made her feel restless. She moved quickly towards the kitchen and opened the cupboard of wine glasses, took one down, then opened the fridge. She pulled out a bottle of cold white wine, poured a glass and carried it to the drawing room. There, she lit the fire and sat down on the cream silk sofa.

As the logs began to spark and the room warmed, she sat sipping her glass of wine.

It would be nice to have someone to talk to, she thought.

Why am I thinking that? I've never been afraid to be alone before, she thought, staring into the fire.

Why do I feel lonely? Is it because I'm older?

She exhaled hard. I've never had these thoughts before, she thought. Never. What is wrong with me? What am I thinking about this for? Verena will be home soon and I shall get supper and find out more about her magic power.

Glenda looked around. Despite the warm fire, the drawing room felt empty.

Outside in the big hallway, the Christmas tree lights twinkled.

But who is here to see them, Glenda thought. Nobody but me.

I hope Stephen is back soon . . .

She sighed. There are so many mistakes I have made, but the biggest was leaving my boy.

What mistakes? she wondered. What am I thinking of?

It feels as if things are changing . . .

Zoe will soon be back in her house with Stephen. Verena will be happy. And I shall be – where?

She smiled as she thought of her son, now a successful City lawyer. A kind man. So different from me, she thought. I wonder how I didn't feel anything for him for all those years. What's changed, I wonder?

As she took another sip of wine, her mind turned to the robin. She sighed heavily.

Why did I do that? Why did I use my power to show Verena – and kill that blasted bird? *Why?*

She hates me now. She didn't like before – but she really hates me. I could see it in her eyes . . .

I'm sure she's got her magic power. I can sense it. Oh, how we could use our power together and wipe the Sprites off the map! That would show them!

But Verena won't do it, she thought, staring at the fire. I can try to force her, like I did with Charles Smythson – but she won't do it.

And then where will I be? Sitting in the south of France – alone. Old and alone. Old and alone and unloved . . .

Glenda laughed a short laugh. Well, what did I expect, she thought. You get back what you give out in life, so they say. I've given out a lot of pain – and now it is coming back to me.

It was always all right, before. I could move on. When I was younger, I had a wonderful career in the ballet. Men asked me to marry them. I made money and travelled the world. All in all, I've had a very comfortable life.

She stared at the flames licking round the pine logs.

What was it Verena had said, as she went out to bury the

robin? '*When you came here to look after me in June, I was so pleased. I thought you'd love me and we'd be friends and have fun together. I'm sorry that hasn't happened.*'

Her words just bounced off me then – but now . . .

She shivered slightly, put down her glass and crossed her arms over her chest.

Now . . . Verena's words touch me in a way I've never felt before. Now I wonder if this way of life is what I really want any more . . .

Glenda Glass stared into the fire.

If Stephen knew what I had done, he may never speak to me again. It would break his heart. It's taken me all these years to connect with him. I was no mother to him when he was younger, but he seems to have forgiven me. He asked me to come and take care of Verena. Why did it take me so long to learn to love him?

She looked down at her watch. Nearly five o'clock – Verena will be home soon, she thought. The Sprites are dropping her back.

I wish she'd come home . . .

I wonder what she has told the girls about her new power? Has she told them anything?

Will she tell them about the robin?

What was it she said about magic power this morning?

'*If this is what having magic power means, then I don't want it.*' That's what she said.

I wonder what I should do . . .

As soon as Verena came through the door ten minutes later,

Glenda knew something had happened.

Her granddaughter's face blazed with anger in a way Glenda had never seen before.

As she locked the front door, Verena strode across the hallway and dumped her coat and bag down on a chair. Then she turned and looked at her grandmother with angry eyes.

'So now I know,' she spat. 'Now I know the truth – and what a despicable, wicked person you are!'

Glenda gasped with surprise. Should she use her magic to stop Verena speaking, she wondered.

But Verena was not going to be stopped. She put up her hand and looked Glenda straight in the eye. 'No, you listen to me for once, Grandma.'

She drew a deep breath and said in the most resolute voice she could muster, '*You've got to give it back, Grandma!*'

Glenda's eyes narrowed.

'They know, you know!' said Verena, her voice rising. 'They *all* know about you stealing Marilyn Sprite's money. I'm amazed Ottalie and Colin haven't told Daddy! At least, Flame and her sisters didn't think he knew – yet.'

Verena clenched her fist. 'How *could* you? How could you do this to the Sprites? Why are you so obsessed with hurting them? What is the *matter* with you?'

Glenda's eyes glinted, her thin lips tightened. She clenched her right fist and began to raise it.

I could shut her up by sending her a bolt of power, she thought.

But it was as if some invisible hand stopped her raising her fist. She could not move it higher. A few seconds later, she lowered it and unclenched her fingers. Verena was still watching her with a look of fury.

Instead of using her power, Glenda turned and walked through to the kitchen. 'It's supper time,' she said.

'Grandma – LISTEN!' shouted Verena, following her.

Glenda opened the fridge and pulled out a plate of raw salmon. She put the fish on the counter and turned to face Verena. Then she hissed, 'Do not EVER speak to me like that again!'

Instead of backing off, Verena came closer. So close that she was standing right in front of her grandmother, her eyes full of pain.

'They've told me about the things you did to them,' she said. 'And it all made sense.'

Glenda raised an eyebrow.

Verena drew a deep breath, then said in a quiet voice, 'And, anyway – I already knew. I overheard your argument with Charles Smythson a few weeks ago.'

She waited as Glenda digested this information.

Glenda looked down and put one hand out on the counter to steady herself.

Verena waited a few seconds, then said, 'Everything the Sprite Sisters told me makes sense, in the light of what he said to you – so I know they're not lying.'

Her beautiful face crumpled, suddenly, and her shoulders sank. 'How *could* you, Grandma? What is it you are trying to prove?'

For the first time in her life, Glenda Glass found she was speechless.

I don't know what to say, she thought. What *is* the answer . . .

She looked up and stared across the kitchen, her thin dancer's body stiff with tension.

Verena waited, silent. She watched as her grandmother's head dropped forward slightly and she leaned on the cabinet, as if weighed down by something heavy.

After a while, Verena said, 'I showed the Sprite Sisters my magic power.'

Glenda turned, slowly. Their eyes met. 'What did you say?'

Verena gasped, aware of the change in her grandmother's face – but her courage held.

'Flame thinks I have the magic power of metal – like an element,' she said, quickly. 'I'm like a super-conductor.'

Glenda stared at her granddaughter. Her eyes grew cold.

Verena drew a sharp breath. 'I'm not going to use my magic power to hurt anyone – ever!' she said, putting her hands on her hips. 'So don't try to make me! If you do, I'll tell Daddy all about you – and he'll send you away and we'll never see you again!'

And with that, she turned and marched out of the kitchen.

At Sprite Towers, Flame and her sisters waited anxiously for Verena to contact them.

'I hope she's all right,' said Marina. 'I thought we'd have heard from her by now.'

'She's been reluctant to call before, as she thought her grandmother would find out,' said Flame. 'I'm sure we'll hear from her soon. She promised she'd let us know.'

And with that, her mobile beeped.

'What does she say?' asked Marina, as they crowded round Flame.

Flame read out Verena's text. '*I told her. She went all quiet. I said we'd tell Daddy if she didn't give your grandmother back the money. Then I ran up to my room.*'

Flame texted back immediately. *Are you okay?*

To which Verena replied, *Yes. Supper in a minute. Xx*

To which Flame replied, *Text after supper to let us know you're okay. And WELL DONE!*

The Sprite Sisters looked at one another. 'Well, there's no turning back now,' said Flame, biting her bottom lip.

'We'd better tell Grandma,' said Marina.

'And check the plan, to see if anything's changed,' added Ash.

That evening, Grandma and the Sprite Sisters sat around the blazing fire in the library. The girls were in their dressing gowns, ready for bed. Mum and Dad had gone out to a party, so for once they could talk uninterrupted.

'Have you heard from Verena since supper?' asked Grandma, her arm over Ariel, who was snuggled up beside her and half asleep.

Flame nodded. 'She said Glenda suggested they eat on trays and watch a film. It meant they didn't need to talk, which was a relief to Verena. She said her grandmother's been very odd, though.'

'Odd?' asked Grandma.

'Yeah – sort of really quiet. And a bit sad.'

Grandma gave a short laugh. 'That doesn't sound much like Glenda!'

'That's what Verena said,' agreed Flame. 'She thought Glenda would be really horrible and get angry – and she didn't.'

Grandma looked towards the fire, silent for a while. Then she said, 'I have a feeling things are going to change.'

'Change?' asked Marina. 'How do you mean, Grandma?'

Grandma eyes looked thoughtful. 'I don't know, love. I just have this feeling something is different, but I don't know where or how.'

At this, Flame looked alert. 'I'll go and get the plan. I wonder if that's changed again.' And she dashed off and up the wide mahogany staircase, taking the stairs two by two, right up to the second floor of the house. A minute later she came back into the library, slightly breathless and holding the little wooden box.

'That was quick!' laughed Grandma.

'Phew!' said Flame, flopping down in front of the fire and pushing back her hair from her face. Laying the wooden box on the rug, she prised open the lid and drew out the plan.

'What's happened?' asked Ash, looking over her shoulder.

'Has it changed?' asked Marina.

Flame gave a big smile. 'Look! The dot has grown – it's become a circle! There's a circle on this plan that wasn't there before – and it's right in the middle of the West Tower!'

'Amazing!' said Marina, peering at the plan. 'I wonder what it means?'

'Oh my goodness!' said Ash, seeing the small black circle which had appeared.

Ariel pulled herself up and rubbed her eyes. 'It means it's time to find the treasure,' she announced, with a big yawn. Then she laid her head down on Grandma's lap and went to sleep in her fluffy pink dressing gown.

As Grandma stroked Ariel's soft, wavy blond hair, she smiled at Flame. 'I think she's right, you know.'

Flame nodded, then looked down at the plan. 'Hm,' she agreed.

'Treasure!' exclaimed Ash.

'It's an important time for the Sprite family,' said Grandma in a quiet voice, as she stared at the fire. 'A lot could happen now.'

CHAPTER EIGHT

FLAME AND MARINA PAY A VISIT

SUNDAY MORNING was cold and dry. The sky was clear and the sun shone through the bare trees.

No snow today by the looks of it, thought Flame, as she drew back her bedroom curtains.

She looked out over the wide rolling lawn. By the edge of the Wild Wood, the old white caravan where they had camped in the summer looked cold and lonely. Archie was lolloping round on the grass carrying a stick in his mouth. Bert was pottering about, sniffing the ground. Dad was already up and walking down to the woodshed, to stock up on firewood.

Only nine days to Christmas, she thought. What fun we shall have!

Her next thought was: I wonder how Verena is getting on at The Oaks?

She turned and picked up the mobile phone lying on her bedside table. There was no text from Verena that morning.

She might still be asleep, thought Flame. Not everybody's an early bird like me.

Drawing her red woolly dressing gown around her, she moved back to the window.

Things are changing – Grandma said so and I can feel it, she thought, staring out. I must use my magic power to see ahead. The plan – I must check the plan.

She moved across to the bookshelf, sat down on the navy carpet and drew out the wooden box from its hiding place.

As soon as she had unfolded the secret plan, she looked for the circle on the West Tower.

There it was! But now a line had appeared across the diameter of the circle. Flame gasped.

As Ash opened the door, Flame turned and said, 'Come and look at this!'

Her younger sister's face was bright with anticipation as she sat down on the carpet in her green dressing gown. 'I wonder where the plan will lead us?'

'To the treasure!' laughed Flame.

'There's a new line across the circle,' said Ash, pointing.

'You spotted it.'

'It's like the beginning of a Crossed Circle – you know the thing Mrs Duggery told us to watch out for?'

'You could be right,' said Flame, taking the plan and looking at it again. 'We'll have to wait and see if more lines cross the circle.'

'I'll bet that's what it is,' said Ash.

They turned to look as Marina and Ariel walked through the door, both yawning.

'It's so cold up here,' said Marina, with a shiver. She wore thick, stripy bed socks and bright yellow pyjamas. 'I hate this cold weather!'

'You're a creature of the sun,' said Flame.

'Too right,' agreed Marina, sitting down beside Ash.

Ariel plopped down in a heap beside Flame. Soft blond hair covered most of her face.

'How can you see where you are going with all that hair covering your eyes?' said Flame, pushing it back from her little sister's face.

Ariel smiled, sleepily. 'I don't need to see. I'm like a bat – I have a special radar that senses when objects are close and I move out of the way.'

'At a much slower speed than a bat,' giggled Ash.

'Ariel the bat!' said Ash, holding out her arms like wings.

'Well, she squeaks like one!' said Marina.

'Very funny,' yawned Ariel. Her big grey eyes opened and she looked around at her sisters. 'So what's up, then?'

'The plan has changed again,' said Flame. 'And I haven't heard from Verena yet.'

'She's probably still asleep,' said Ash.

'I expect her house is warmer than ours,' said Marina. 'Gawd know why Mum and Dad can't put more heating on.'

'They're worried about the environment,' said Ash.

'And trying to save money,' added Marina.

'Well, it costs a fortune to heat Sprite Towers,' said Ash, bridling.

'One day they'll find me up in my room frozen solid – then they'll be sorry,' said Marina, pouting.

'It's nice and warm in the kitchen,' said Ariel. 'And there's toast and marmalade and yummy things for breakfast.'

'Hm, breakfast,' said Marina. 'That sounds a good idea.' She jumped up suddenly, exclaimed, 'Last one down's a sissy!' and ran out of the room.

And they all raced downstairs to the kitchen.

By mid-morning, Flame was anxious. 'I still haven't heard from Verena,' she said to Marina. They were sitting in the library, wrapping up presents for Mum.

In the kitchen, Mum was baking bread for the week and Grandma was preparing the Sunday roast lunch. Dad was down in the vegetable garden, digging up parsnips. Ash and Ariel were cleaning out the rabbit hutches by the stables.

'Oh Lord, this is endless,' said Marina, looking round at the big pile of presents that still needed wrapping.

'At least it's warm in here by the fire,' said Flame, pulling out a line of Sellotape and sticking it down.

'That's true,' said Marina, cutting a new length of wrapping paper.

'What shall we do about Verena?' asked Flame.

'What can we do?'

'Dunno. Go round there? Make sure she's all right?' said Flame, frowning.

'How would we go round?'

'On our bikes,' said Flame, putting down her present on the floor. Her face had a look of sudden concentration.

'Mum will have a fit,' said Marina. 'We're meant to be helping today.'

'We are helping – and this wouldn't take long,' said Flame. 'We could just whizz over there and come straight back. It's not far.'

'What would we say? We can't just disappear.'

Flame put down her parcel and stared at the fire. 'That we're worried about Verena. I don't know why she is not answering my texts.'

'She didn't call us before, if you remember,' said Marina.

'Yes, but that was before she had told her grandmother that she knew everything. She could be in real danger now and unable to reach us. I'm really worried.'

Marina caught her gaze. 'I know you are.'

Just then, Flame's phone beeped the arrival of a text. 'It's Verena,' she said, looking at the screen. 'She says she's just woken up and she's trying to avoid talking to her grandmother. She says Glenda's being "odd" and she feels uneasy with her.'

'She said Glenda was being "odd" yesterday evening. I wonder what she means?'

Flame looked at Marina. 'I think we ought to go round there as a show of strength – so that Glenda knows Verena's not alone. Knowing that everyone knows about her stealing

Grandma's money must have rattled Glenda. If we show up, it might just stop her trying to influence Verena and push her towards dark power.'

'It may, but Glenda is a tough and heartless woman.' Marina stood up. 'Okay, let's go then. Better put jackets and scarves on.'

'And gloves,' added Flame. 'It's cold out there.'

The two elder Sprite Sisters grabbed their outside gear and went through to the kitchen to tell their mother. She was busy on the phone in the dining room, however, so they told their grandmother of their plans.

'Is that wise?' said Grandma. 'You could put yourselves in a dangerous spot. Can't you wait for her to call you?'

'We're worried, Grandma,' said Flame. 'We just want to see Verena, to make sure she is okay.'

'Has Glenda threatened her?' asked Grandma.

'She's keeping out of her grandmother's way as much as possible,' said Flame. 'She says Glenda is being "odd".'

Grandma sighed. 'I'd rather you didn't, but if you really feel Verena needs help then go. But be quick and stay together. Take care that Glenda does not use her magic on you.'

'We will take care,' said Flame, kissing her grandmother on the cheek.

'Go on then, hurry up,' said Grandma. 'I'll tell your mother. Just make sure you're back for lunch and take care on the road – and wear your bike helmets!'

'We will,' replied the sisters, as they sped out of the kitchen door.

They ran over the lawn to collect their bikes from the shed in one of the old stables.

'Where are you going?' asked Ash, as they ran past.

'Can we come, too?' asked Ariel, when Marina had explained their plan.

'No, it's too complicated and Mum will get suspicious if we all go,' said Flame. 'For God's sake don't tell her why we've really gone over there.'

'But what about if Glenda uses her magic power on you?' asked Ash, her brown eyes worried. 'You could get hurt.'

'We'll be okay,' said Marina, as they yanked their bikes out of the shed and put on their helmets.

A moment later, the two girls were speeding down the long driveway of Sprite Towers.

It took them twelve minutes to cycle along the narrow, winding country lane to The Oaks, a mile away. At the big iron gates, they stopped and looked across to the house.

'So what do we say when Glenda opens the front door?' asked Marina. 'She could use her power to blast us to smithereens.'

They stared over the wide gravel driveway, wondering what to do.

Flame glanced up. 'Verena's seen us – look, she's up at that window.'

She waved at Verena.

They waited. Thirty seconds later, Verena opened the front door and beckoned them forward.

The two sisters got off their bicycles. As they pushed their cycles towards the wide oak front door, the tall figure of

Glenda Glass appeared behind Verena. Her face looked hard as stone.

Flame and Marina kept a little way back.

'Hello,' they said.

Verena ran out to greet them, wearing just a T-shirt and jeans. 'Hi!' she said, all smiles.

Glenda moved into the doorway. 'Good morning,' she said. She looked at Flame and said, 'To what do we owe this unexpected visit?'

'We came to see Verena,' replied Flame.

'Well, I didn't think you'd come to see *me*,' replied Glenda, with a cold smile. She walked forward slightly, as if fixing Flame in her sights. The two sisters instinctively moved closer – and Verena moved to stand in front of them.

Flame and Marina watched Glenda warily.

Verena turned to look at her grandmother. Don't you dare, her expression said.

Glenda ignored Verena and raised her right hand slightly, her eyes glinting. Seeing this, Flame and Marina started. Their hands began to tingle, ready to use their magic power if need be.

Glenda watched the Sprite Sisters. The Sprite Sisters watched Glenda.

Verena stood stock still, her eyes focused on her grandmother.

For a few seconds nobody moved. Glenda's hand stayed suspended in mid-air.

Then – suddenly – she turned and walked into the house, leaving the door a little ajar.

The girls laughed with relief.

'I wondered what she was going to do,' said Flame.

'So did I!' laughed Verena.

'Thank heavens *that* is over,' said Marina, with a grin.

Verena shivered. 'It's cold out here,' she laughed. 'But it's so good to see you! Thank you for coming over.'

'Are you all right?' asked Flame. 'We've been worried about you.'

'Has your grandmother said anything about how to use your power?' asked Marina, looking towards the door.

Verena shook her head. 'Not so far – but you know how quickly she changes. And when she does get nasty, she gets really nasty. I'm just keeping out of her way – that's why I was up so late this morning.'

'You can't hide from her till your parents get home,' said Flame. 'They won't be back for another eight days.'

Verena looked at the ground, wrapped her arms around her chest and rubbed her hands up and down her arms. 'Perhaps I could come over to stay with you this week some time?'

'I'll ask Mum,' said Flame.

Verena looked up, her face earnest. 'I meant what I said to my grandmother, you know.'

Flame and Marina waited.

'I'm not – ever – going to use my magic power for anything dark or harmful,' said Verena.

'She's bound to try to make you,' said Marina, with worried eyes. 'And you're all alone . . .'

'What did you mean by Glenda being "odd"?' asked Flame.

Verena looked round at the door, now shivering hard with cold. 'There's something *different* about her – I dunno. It's funny. I've not seen her like this before. She hasn't said anything, but I get this feeling she's lonely – or something like that. She's so *quiet* all of a sudden, and a couple of times her face has looked – well, sort of *sad*.'

'Sad?' said Marina. 'Doesn't sound like Glenda Glass.'

'That's what I thought,' agreed Verena.

Flame was just about to tell Verena about the secret plan changing again, when the front door opened and Glenda Glass appeared. 'Verena, you will catch a cold out here, dressed like that,' she said. 'Now either put a jacket on or come inside.'

She gave Flame and Marina a hard look, then turned to go back into the house.

'It's okay – we've got to go back for lunch now,' said Flame, pulling her bike towards her.

Verena nodded. 'Thanks so much for coming over,' she said, as the two sisters got on their bicycles.

Verena waved as they cycled out of the gate, then went back into the house.

In the hallway, Glenda was waiting. 'What was that all about?'

'They came to see if I was all right,' said Verena, closing the front door.

'And why wouldn't you be "all right"?'

Verena looked at her grandmother's cold eyes, then down at the stone floor. 'I suppose . . . they wanted us both to know that I am not alone.'

Glenda watched Verena silently.

Verena waited a few seconds, then looked up and said, 'Things are changing, Grandma. We have to change with them.'

'Hrumph,' snorted Glenda, with a look of derision. 'Change, my foot!' And she turned and walked towards the kitchen.

As Verena went up to her room and Flame and Marina pedalled home as quickly as they could, Glenda gazed out of the kitchen window, her mind unsettled. Close by was the bird table, on which she had killed the robin two days before.

Since then, every time she looked out of this window, she had thought of the little bird.

Thinking of the robin reminded her of Verena's words. *'When you came here to look after me in June, I was so pleased.'*

Verena is not pleased now, she thought. She hates me and she wants me to go. I can see it in her eyes.

What is happening to me? Why do I care what Verena thinks? All my life, I've never cared what anybody felt about me.

She looked down at her hands. They were still trembling.

I was tempted to use my magic on those damn Sprite Sisters, she thought. Why did they come poking round here? And Verena was so pleased to see them! Huh!

She turned away from the window, looked around the big empty kitchen.

Another eight days until Stephen and Zoe are home, she

thought. Then what do I do? Wait until Marilyn Sprite gets the police to arrest me for stealing her money? How did they find it? I hid it so well . . .

What was the other thing Verena said? *'You've got to give it back.'*

Everything is beginning to feel out of control, she thought, conscious of her heart pumping hard in her thin chest.

I had it all so well planned – but nothing has worked out the way I intended.

For the first time in my life, I feel scared . . .

CHAPTER NINE

EXCUSES

'WHAT WAS so pressing that you had to dash off in such a hurry?' asked Mum, as Flame and Marina came back in through the kitchen door.

'We were worried about Verena,' replied Flame, pulling off her jacket.

'Why – what's happened?'

'She's not very happy – being alone with her grand-mother,' said Flame.

'We know that – but what made you rush off like that?' persisted Mum.

'She wasn't answering our calls.'

'She said Glenda was being a bit odd,' added Marina, taking off her gloves.

Mum frowned. 'Odd? What do you mean?'

'Even more quiet than usual, apparently,' said Flame, quickly.

Marina stepped forward and looked at Mum. 'We were just a bit worried about Verena, that's all. She's so alone.'

'I know – and it's kind of you to be concerned for her,' agreed Mum, 'but her parents will be back in a few days, so you shouldn't worry. How was she anyway?'

'Very glad to see us,' said Marina.

'Okay,' said Mum, satisfied. 'Go and hang up your things. Lunch is nearly ready. Marina, can you set the table, please? And Flame . . .'

She was about to ask Flame to ring the bell outside the back door to summon Dad, Ash and Ariel for lunch, but the eldest Sprite Sister had already left the kitchen and was mounting the wide mahogany staircase to her room.

Mum blinked in surprise at her sudden exit. She turned to Grandma, who was spooning roast potatoes into a serving dish and said, 'Flame's been dashing upstairs a lot the last few days. I wonder what she keeps going up there for?'

'I'm pleased she and Verena seem to be getting on so well – makes a big change,' said Grandma, hoping to steer Mum away from why Flame kept going upstairs. 'They were deadly enemies not so long ago.'

'Yes, that's true,' agreed Mum, turning to stir the gravy, which was bubbling away on top of the Aga. Beside this, keeping warm on a big white plate, was the joint of roast beef.

As preparations for lunch went on in the kitchen, Flame sat

on her bedroom floor looking at the secret plan.

It's changed again, she thought, seeing another line cross the circle. The second line had divided the circle into quarters.

I *knew* something was happening. I could feel it.

I wonder why? What's happened this morning that could be connected to the plan?

Nothing particular has happened here. Unless . . .

She looked up and across the room, her brow furrowed with concentration.

Unless . . . it's something to do with our connection to *Verena* . . .

When did the first mark appear? Wednesday – it was Wednesday night, when we were sitting on my bed. And when did Verena's hands start to tingle? That was Wednesday, too, so she told us.

Flame's face broke into a smile as a sudden realisation hit her.

Oh my goodness – I wonder if there's a connection between us, the plan and Verena? If that were the case, it would mean the magic is not just about Sprite Towers. It's about the whole Sprite *family*.

That would make sense, she thought, biting her bottom lip and staring at the plan.

So, if it's changing quickly now – what does that signify? That things are changing here – or at The Oaks? What's going on?

With a sense of excitement, Flame carefully folded up the secret plan and put it back in its wooden box behind the books. Then she ran back down to the kitchen, to take her place at the lunch table.

Marina, Ash and Ariel looked at her with a sense of curiosity. 'Tell you later,' she whispered to them, with a smile.

At the end of the long oak table, Dad carved the big joint of roast beef and laid the slices on the plates, one by one. In the centre of the table were dishes of home-grown vegetables – roast potatoes, parsnips, onions, steamed carrots and Mum's special spicy cabbage, along with a big jug of gravy and a bowl of horseradish sauce.

'It looks and smells wonderful,' said Marina. 'I'm so hungry!'

Within a few minutes, everyone had been served and was tucking into a plate of delicious food. Under the table, Archie wandered around looking for crumbs.

'Basket!' said Dad, firmly, pointing to it. Archie looked at him with baleful eyes and went back to his basket. 'Good boy,' said Dad.

For a while they talked about Christmas and all the things they had to do. Then, somehow, Verena came up in the conversation. It was only one step from there to Glenda.

Mum looked over at Marina and asked, 'What did you mean by Glenda being "odd"?'

Marina looked at Flame. 'Er – well, Verena said they had never talked much, but now Glenda is completely silent.'

'I expect she's wondering how life at The Oaks will be when Zoe gets back in a few days,' said Mum. And for a little while they talked about the impending change.

Then it happened.

One minute Ariel was eating quietly, a contented look on

her face. The next she blurted out, 'I think Glenda's being odd because Verena told her she had to give Grandma her money back.'

Flame, Marina and Ash looked at one another in horror, then at Mum. Had she heard this?

Mum stopped eating and turned to Ariel, sitting on her right side. 'What did you say?'

Ariel looked up at Mum, as if awoken from a dream. 'What?'

'What did you say about Glenda giving Grandma's money back?'

Ariel blinked. She looked quickly round the table. Grandma and her sisters were all glaring at her.

Dad sat forward and looked at Mum at the other end of the table. 'What's this?' he asked.

Mum looked at Dad and said in a tone of disbelief. 'Ariel has just announced that Verena has told Glenda she has to give back Marilyn's money!'

'What?' spluttered Dad.

'Oh Gawd, here we go . . .' muttered Flame under her breath. She looked across at Grandma, who had stopped eating and was wiping her mouth with a napkin.

'Ariel, how do you know about Grandma's money?' asked Mum. 'Your father and I have never spoken about this matter to you girls.'

Ariel sat like a startled rabbit, her eyes wide. 'Verena told us,' she said in a small voice.

Mum looked around the table at her daughters. '*And how does Verena know?*'

There was silence.

Mum looked at Dad.

Flame looked at Grandma, then at Marina, then at Ash. What should they say?

Just as Grandma was about to speak, Ariel blurted again. 'She heard Charles arguing with Glenda!'

Mum turned to face Ariel and said, in a deliberate voice, 'She heard *Charles* arguing with *Glenda*? What do you mean she "heard Charles arguing with Glenda"? What has Charles got to do with this? How would *he* know about Grandma's money?'

There was complete silence. Mum's face looked like thunder. Dad looked completely bewildered.

Flame's heart pounded in her chest. How could they explain the truth about Charles?

Then Grandma said in a clear, firm voice, 'Because I told him.'

Everyone looked round at Grandma. She sat tall and straight in her chair and looked at Mum. 'When Charles was here in the summer, I told him as I thought he might be able to help me. He is Glenda's nephew, as you know.'

'You never told us you'd spoken to Charles about this!' said Mum, surprised.

Grandma gave a small shrug. 'I apologise, Ottalie – I must have just forgotten about it.'

Flame, Marina and Ash each breathed a sigh of relief. Ariel sat stock still on her chair.

'Did Charles help, Ma?' asked Dad.

'He was able to tell me he thought she had been married

four times – and that the last husband was a French lawyer,' she replied.

Mum exhaled and put both hands flat on the table. She looked around at her daughters, then fixed her gaze on Flame. 'Let's just get this clear, please. Ariel says that Verena has told Glenda to *give back* the money. Is that correct?'

Flame looked at Mum. 'Yes.'

'And this is perhaps why Glenda is being "odd"?'

'I think it could be.'

Mum sat back in her chair, folded her arms across her chest and looked over at Dad, as if to say, *What next?*

Dad scratched his chin – a sure sign that he was troubled. Everyone had stopped eating.

'Hm,' said Dad, slowly.

Mum gave a sharp laugh. 'Hm, indeed.'

'Well, at least now Glenda knows we all know,' said Marina. 'I think Verena was very brave to confront her.'

'Yes, she was,' said Dad. 'And it's a good thing that it is out in the open.' He looked round at Grandma. 'How do you feel about it, Ma?'

'I think, on balance, that it's a good thing,' she said.

'Will Glenda go to prison?' asked Ariel.

Dad pursed his lips. 'She could do. It's a serious crime she's committed.'

'But wouldn't Stephen and Zoe and Verena be upset?' asked Ash.

Dad looked down the table at Mum, then scratched his chin again. 'Hm,' he said. 'It would be very tricky.'

As the Sprite family thought about this, they picked up

their knives and forks and resumed their lunch. Mum got up to warm the gravy. Grandma handed round the vegetable dishes and Dad carved a few more slices of meat.

For the next few minutes they ate quietly with thoughtful faces.

As soon as lunch was finished and the clearing up completed, the Sprite Sisters dashed up to Flame's room.

They flopped down on the navy carpet.

'Phew, that was close,' said Marina, with a sigh.

'Ariel, you are the limit! You did it again!' said Flame.

'I can't help it,' said Ariel, hugging her legs and resting her chin on her knees. 'Sometimes things just come out.'

'Well, you ought to be more careful,' said Flame. 'One of these days you're going to *really* get us in trouble. If Mum ever found out about our magic, that would be *it*.'

'What do you mean?' asked Ash.

Flame gave a short, hard laugh. 'Do you remember how Mum reacted to the ghost? As soon as it had gone, she denied it existed! She reckoned it was all nonsense! She does not believe in magic. If she ever found out about us, she'd have a complete fit.'

'She wouldn't believe us,' said Ash.

'And if she did, she'd probably try to stop us using our magic powers,' said Marina.

'And if she found us using them, it may weaken our powers as she's not a Sprite – remember,' added Flame.

They were silent. Then Ash said, 'Meanwhile, Mrs Duggery wants us to find the treasure.'

'Right under Mum's nose,' added Marina.

'Exactly!' said Flame.

'Let's see the plan, then,' said Marina.

A minute later, Marina, Ash and Ariel huddled round Flame, who held the open plan in her hands. As they leaned over, she spluttered, 'Oh, my goodness!'

'What?' echoed Marina and Ash.

'What is it?' said Ariel, trying to see.

'Look – look there!' said Flame. 'The crossed circle has got two more lines across it.'

'Yes, look, there's a third line,' murmured Ash, with a look of surprise.

'Making six sections,' said Flame.

'But I thought there were only two lines on the Crossed Circle motif around the house and on the magic box,' said Marina. 'Two lines, four sections.'

'So did I – but not any longer,' said Flame, raising her eyebrows.

'Weird,' whispered Ariel. For a moment they were silent. Then Ariel gulped, 'What does it mean? Why has it changed?'

'I don't know, pumpkin,' said Flame.

'Looks like there's a line missing,' said Ash, pointing at the plan.

'Yes,' agreed Flame.

'A fourth line crossing the circle would form eight sections,' said Marina.

They were silent as they thought on this. Then Ariel piped up, 'I can understand four sections makes sense because there are four of us – and that makes one section for each of us.

But, eight – what does eight mean?'

'You mean who would that be?' asked Ash.

Ariel nodded. 'Yes, I s'pose so.'

Flame frowned as she stared at the plan. 'I don't know,' she said.

Meanwhile, downstairs in the library, Mum, Dad and Grandma were sitting by the fire. This was the time on Sunday afternoon when they drank coffee and read the newspapers. As usual, Bert sat beneath Grandma's feet. Little Archie lay sprawled out on the carpet, asleep for once.

Today, however, Mum was not reading the paper. She was staring at the fire.

'What's up, love?' asked Dad, looking up.

She smiled across at him. 'Oh, I was just thinking about the girls and what they said about Verena.'

'And?'

Mum shook her head. 'I just have the feeling we haven't heard the whole story.' She looked across at Grandma. 'What do you think, Marilyn?'

'About the girls?'

Mum nodded, but before Grandma could answer she said, 'They've been very secretive – don't you think?'

Grandma smiled and leaned down to stroke Bert's long silky ears.

Dad gave a short laugh. 'They're *always* secretive!'

'It's just a feeling I've got,' said Mum, with a small smile. 'Sometimes I get the feeling that they're hiding something from us – you know?'

Dad laughed again. 'All kids hide things from their parents! They live in their own private worlds. Look at Ariel, she's away with the fairies most of the time!'

Mum frowned. 'It's Flame I was really thinking about.'

Dad laughed. 'Teenager! Aren't I right, Ma?'

Grandma smiled at him, then looked at Mum. 'Flame is deep thinking,' she agreed. 'But she's a lovely girl – you shouldn't worry so.'

Mum put down her cup of coffee on the table. 'I think I'll just go upstairs and have a chat to Flame,' she said, standing up. 'I'd like to find out a bit more about Verena.'

Grandma drew a sharp breath. I hope the girls aren't doing anything with their magic powers, she thought.

'Okay, love,' said Dad, turning the page on his newspaper.

What is it, Mum wondered, as she climbed the wide mahogany staircase. As a musician and a singer, Ottalie Sprite's senses were finely tuned. Above all, she had the sharpest hearing. Today, something was jarring. It was as if a note was being played slightly out of tune.

There's something not right, she thought, as she reached the second floor of the big house.

She walked quietly along the corridor to Flame's room. Outside the door, she listened.

The girls are all in there chattering, she thought. With that, she gave a small knock and opened the door.

It was something about the way all four girls *completely* froze that made Mum suspicious.

'What is that you are looking at?' she asked. 'Show me.'

CHAPTER TEN

DAD'S AWAKENING

MUM HELD out her hand and looked steadily at Flame.

The Sprite Sisters sat completely still on the carpet, their eyes fixed on Mum. The silence was awesome. Mum looked around the room. The only light came from the lamp on Flame's bedside table.

'Flame, give me the piece of paper you are holding, please,' repeated Mum.

Flame remained still. She stared at Mum, her eyes wide, her mouth slightly open.

As Mum looked down at the other girls, she saw the same expression on their faces. Horror. Amazement. Confusion.

None of them had moved an inch. None of them had so much as blinked.

Mum took a step back and looked at each of her daughters again. Whatever is it that has such a hold on them, she wondered, feeling a rising sense of panic.

Then irritation took over. 'Flame, give me that thing NOW!'

Marina, Ash and Ariel spun round to look at Flame. 'No!' they whispered. 'Don't show her!'

Flame looked up at Mum, her green eyes blazing. 'No,' she replied and lowered her hand to the carpet.

Mum put her hands on her hips, looked up to the ceiling and gave a short, hard laugh. 'Whatever is going on here? I demand to see what it is that you are all trying to keep from me!'

As she said this, she was aware that Marina, Ash and Ariel were moving closer to Flame – as if making a circle around her to protect her.

Mum stared at her daughters in amazement.

The Sprite Sisters stared at her.

Mum held out her hand again. *'Flame, give me the piece of paper!'*

'No,' repeated Flame.

For a few seconds, Mum glared at Flame. 'Right!' she said, then turned and walked quickly out of the room. At the top of the staircase, she stopped and shouted down to the hallway two floors below.

'COLIN!' Then again, 'COLIN!'

A moment later, Dad appeared in the hallway. 'What's the matter?' he shouted, looking up with a worried face.

'Come up here, please – right now!'

Dad bounded up the stairs. Grandma followed.

'What's happened?' he said, puffing at the top.

Mum's face was angry. 'The girls are behaving very strangely. They've got something – and they will not show me what it is.'

'So?'

Mum looked at Dad in exasperation *'So, I want them to show me! For heaven's sake, Colin!'*

'What do you want me to do?' he asked, as Grandma reached the landing and came up behind them.

'Get them to give it to us, of course!' exclaimed Mum. Dad looked round at Grandma, noted the tension in her face, then walked towards Flame's bedroom.

As he opened the door, he saw his four daughters huddled together on the floor, their faces white.

'What's going on?' he asked, looking down at them.

Ash got up and came to his side. 'Please, Dad, just leave us be,' she said, softly. 'It's nothing nasty. It's just something private, between us.'

Dad smiled down at her, stroking her tufty chestnut hair. He was about to say okay and leave them be, when Mum piled in behind him.

Although small, blond and pretty, Mum could be absolutely terrifying at times. This was one of those moments. *'Colin!'* she said, sharply.

Dad shrugged at Ash, then looked down at Flame and held out his hand. 'Come on,' he said. 'Time to hand it over.'

In the doorway, Grandma waited anxiously. Flame looked across at her. Grandma nodded, as if to say, *Give it to him.*

Flame exhaled hard, then handed the secret plan to Dad.

As she did this, Ash slumped back down beside her sisters. Ariel started crying. Marina put her arm around her.

Dad looked down at his daughters, then at Mum – then opened the piece of paper in his hand.

'Ma, would you turn on the light, please,' he said.

Grandma flicked down the switch beside the door, then moved into the room.

Dad stood under the light hanging from the ceiling in the centre of Flame's room. In his hand was the piece of heavy white paper, the size of a small letter. Beside him, Mum peered over his arm. 'What is it?' she asked.

An architect, Dad recognised what he was looking at in an instant. 'It's the section plans of each floor of Sprite Towers.'

Mum looked up at him, surprised.

Dad gazed at the plan with a look of intense curiosity. 'It's old,' he murmured. 'And it's got some weird markings. See these lines, numbers and symbols going in all directions?'

Mum looked at him again – and waited.

Dad rubbed his chin, then looked at Flame. 'Where did you get this?' he asked.

On the carpet, Flame hugged her legs. Her deep copper hair hung like a curtain over her face. Muffled sobs came from Ariel. Marina and Ash stared silently at the carpet.

Dad waited, but no answer came.

As Mum was about to speak, Grandma said in a firm voice, 'Why don't we all go and talk about this downstairs.'

Dad turned to her. 'Good idea, Ma.'

As he and Mum turned towards the door, Grandma

moved forward towards her granddaughters. As they stood up, she put her arms around them. 'It'll be all right,' she said, softly.

'But it won't!' sobbed Ariel.

Mum and Dad glanced at one another in astonishment.

'What is this all about, I wonder?' asked Mum, as they walked along the corridor. 'I've never seen the girls so upset before.'

Dad sighed. 'I don't know, but I have the feeling you may have opened a can of worms.'

'Me?' said Mum, as they began to walk down the staircase.

Dad was silent. He was thinking about the hurried, old-fashioned writing on the plan; the letters *E*, *S*, *W* and *N* that he had noted on each of the sections; the dotted line across the East Tower. He was wondering about the purpose of the plan.

And, as he wondered, something deep within him stirred.

As he rounded the first-floor landing, he had the sudden thought that some of the Sprites were different. He wasn't different, he didn't think – and he had no idea who was. But he'd heard enough stories about the family history of magic power to sense that the piece of paper in his hand might take him and Mum into unchartered waters. And, if he knew anything about his wife, she would not be happy.

And his daughters: why did they look *so* frightened?

With a sense of trepidation, he turned to Mum beside him and said, 'Be patient with the girls, love – please. They're all very upset.'

Mum bridled. 'I can see that, Colin!'

Dad bit his lip, took her hand firmly and they walked

round the hallway to the library.

At the top of the stairs, Grandma and the Sprite Sisters began to make their way down.

'What do we *say*?' asked Flame.

'Tell them that you found the plan in a wooden box that Ash bought at the village fête last summer,' replied Grandma.

'But they'll want to know what the plan means,' said Flame. 'You saw how curious Dad was.'

Grandma sighed. It's not him I'm worried about, she thought.

'Well, you'll just have to be honest,' said Grandma. 'Answer their questions, but tell them as little as possible. And don't lie.'

Flame groaned. 'This is just *awful*.'

'They might just be satisfied that we were having a treasure hunt,' said Ash.

'On the other hand, they might not give us back the plan – and then what?' said Marina.

'Oh, don't say that!' said Ash.

'Come on, heads up, walk tall,' said Grandma, as they got to the hallway.

It was half past three when the Sprite family gathered in the library. Outside it was almost dark, so Mum drew the curtains over the two long windows. Dad stoked up the fire. Mum and Dad sat down on one of the sofas that ran at right angles to the fire.

Grandma and the Sprite Sisters sat opposite, on the other. As it was a bit of a squash, Ash sat on one of the arms. Ariel moved as close as she could to Grandma.

Mum smiled across at Ariel and patted the sofa. 'Come and sit over here next to me.'

Ariel shook her head. 'I'm all right here.'

'Okay,' said Mum, slightly hurt.

As Mum poured the tea and handed around plates of cake, Dad was looking at the secret plan. His face had a look of fascination.

The Sprite Sisters sat silent, with long faces.

When everybody was settled, Dad looked over at his daughters and said, 'This is really interesting! Where did you find it?'

Marina, Ash and Ariel waited for Flame to answer. She sat up straight and leaned forward. 'Ash bought a small wooden box at the summer fête and this was inside.'

'Why didn't you show us?' asked Dad.

Flame shrugged. 'Dunno – we just didn't.'

Mum looked at Ash. 'Was that the little box you bought from my bric-a-brac stall?'

Ash nodded. 'I paid one pound for it.'

Dad smiled. 'I remember! Charles was here and he was very interested in that box. It was locked though, so we couldn't see what was inside. Where is it, Ash? Have you got it?'

Ash looked across at Flame.

'I'd love to see it,' said Dad. 'Can you get it?'

Flame looked round at Grandma. She gave Flame a nod that said, 'You'll have to.'

'I'll go and get it,' said Flame, standing up.

Flame climbed the stairs with a sense of foreboding and a heavy heart. I'll just bring the box, she thought. I'll take out the things inside.

But when she took out the box from its hiding place and opened the lid, she had the strong sense that the things inside – the two old photographs, the four dried rosebuds, George's letter, the little key – should remain in the box.

They belong here, together. Where else would I put them?

Flame stared into the box. The rosebuds, key and the photographs, yes. But George's letter? There's no way we could explain that away . . .

Oh dear, what shall I do?

What was it Grandma said as we were coming downstairs? Be honest. That's what she said.

Flame gave a long sigh, then shut the lid on the box. She stood up, and with the box in her right hand, she walked back down to the library.

As she came through the hallway, she was struck by the quiet in the house. Normally if her family had been having tea by the fire there would have been the sound of chattering and laughter. Not today. Today, everyone was quiet.

'Ah, there you are,' said Dad, looking up from the plan. Mum sat beside him, sipping her tea.

At the end of the sofa, she stopped and looked down at her grandmother and sisters. Her grandmother gave her a smile of encouragement. Her sisters looked pale-faced and anxious.

Flame leaned over and handed the box to Dad. As he took

it, he placed the plan down on the coffee table in front of him. Marina, Ash and Ariel eyed the plan.

Flame sat back down on the sofa.

'Yes, this *is* the box,' said Dad, with a smile. 'You threw it out – remember, Ottalie?'

Mum grimaced. What she perceived as uncluttering the house, Dad saw as throwing away priceless treasures. In this instance, he had been right.

Dad drew his finger around the Crossed Circle carved into the wooden lid. 'That motif is all over this house,' he said, thoughtfully. 'There must be some connection.'

The girls exchanged glances and held their breath as Dad opened the lid.

Mum leaned forward and looked in. 'Dried rosebuds,' she said. 'And an envelope.'

'And two old photographs.'

'And that little key down there,' said Mum, pointing.

Dad looked up at Flame. 'And you found the plan in here?'

She nodded.

'This looks like a letter,' said Mum, lifting it out.

'Oh no,' groaned Marina. Ariel snuggled closer to Grandma. Ash and Flame looked at Grandma with anxious eyes.

Mum held up the stiff white envelope. '*The Sprite Sisters, Sprite Towers*,' she said, reading the elegant, old-fashioned handwriting. She looked over at her daughters. 'Who is this from?'

They were silent. She looked around at Dad, who had been studying the photographs.

'See what's inside the envelope,' he suggested.

Carefully, Mum pulled out the letter and glanced across at her daughters. Never before had she seen them look so tense. What is going on, she wondered again, opening out the two small sheets of stiff white paper.

For a few seconds, Mum perused the letter in silence. Then she turned to Dad, her face white with shock, and spluttered, 'This letter . . . this letter is dated 1917!'

'1917?'

'It's addressed to "*The Sprite Sisters, Sprite Towers*"!'

'Perhaps there were other Sprite Sisters?' said Dad, putting down the photograph.

'Not called Flame, Marina, Ash and Ariel, there weren't!'

'Perhaps it's a fake letter,' said Dad – but one look across at his daughters was enough to dispel that notion. He could see the tension in their faces.

Mum frowned, as she studied the letter. 'It says you have to find the wooden box to *unlock the secret of Sprite Towers*.' She looked up at Flame. 'What does that mean?'

Flame looked at her, silent.

Mum looked at the letter again. 'What does he mean about the power of the house? Why do you have to guard this plan with your lives? *What does this all mean?*'

Mum looked round at her daughters. They looked back at her. Nobody spoke.

With a face half bewildered and half angry, Mum handed Dad the letter.

'Where did you get this, girls?' he asked, his voice full of concern.

The Sprite Sisters stared across at their parents with a sense of complete dread.

Then Grandma sat forward. 'Ash found it behind the portrait of Mim Sprite – you remember you took it down from the wall in the summer, the day the caravan arrived?'

'You knew about this, Ma?' said Dad, with a look of astonishment.

'Yes, Colin, I did.'

Dad looked at Grandma again, scratched his head and blew out hard. Mum was staring at Grandma.

'Well – well, let's read it then,' said Dad. He was silent as he perused the letter. 'Who is George Sprite?'

'He was Sidney Sprite's second son,' said Grandma. 'He died at the Front in 1917, aged nineteen.'

Dad laughed. 'But that's years before the girls were born! How would he know to write to them?'

As he said this, he looked across at his mother and met her clear green eyes.

It was then that it really hit him. It was as if some deep part of him, which had been asleep all his life, suddenly awoke.

I wonder if this is part of the Sprite magic, he thought. I know it's supposed to run through the family. But my mother? *My daughters?*

His mouth dropped open as he gawped at his mother. Then he repeated in a stuttering voice, 'You – *knew* – about – this, Ma?'

Grandma looked at him with a level eye. 'Yes, dear, I did.'

For a few seconds, Dad held her gaze. Then he said, 'Ah,' very quietly.

Frantically, Mum looked from Grandma to Dad and back. *'Will someone please tell me what is going on?'* she said, her voice rising in frustration.

Dad was speechless. He turned to stare at the fire. Grandma and the Sprite Sisters waited, their heads lowered.

The silence hung in the air.

Mum looked from daughter to husband to mother-in-law, then said in a loud voice, 'TELL ME WHAT IS GOING ON!'

CHAPTER ELEVEN

REVELATIONS ABOUT MAGIC

THE SPRITE Sisters huddled closer to their grandmother on the sofa.

On the sofa opposite, Dad leaned over to Mum and took her hand. 'I think we need to give the girls a chance to explain.'

'Well, that's what I want!' she replied, sharply. 'None of this makes any sense whatsoever.'

Grandma leaned forward. 'Can I make a suggestion?'

'By all means,' replied Dad.

'That we take a break for a few minutes, to go to the loo and make a fresh pot of tea.'

'Good idea,' agreed Dad.

'Okay,' said Mum. She stood up, then leaned down to pick

up the tray of some of the tea things and walked towards the door.

'I'll bring the other things,' said Grandma.

The Sprite Sisters dashed out of the library, past Mum. Dad waited as Grandma picked up the plate with the fruit-cake. Now alone in the room, he said, 'Ma?'

She looked up. 'Yes, dear?'

Dad rubbed his chin. 'Is this, er, is this something to do with the Sprite family magic?'

Grandma gave him a surprised smile. 'Why do you ask that, dear?'

'Well, er, I don't exactly know,' said Dad. 'I had this feeling that the plan was . . . well, it's strange and rather wonderful. And . . . it . . .occurred to me that this . . . this was something to do with the family "magic" that I've heard about.'

Grandma looked at him with her clear green eyes. 'Try to keep an open mind, dear.'

'Ah – so I was right,' said Dad. He gave a short laugh. 'Hm. An open mind . . . Sounds like this could be challenging . . .'

Grandma nodded. 'Ottalie may need some help under-standing it.'

Dad rubbed his chin again.

'I'll go and help her with the tea,' said Grandma. 'And remember – an open mind.'

Outside the door Flame was waiting, her face pale.

She grabbed her grandmother's arm. 'I *must* speak to you!' she whispered. They walked to the dining room and shut the door.

'This is awful!' moaned Flame. 'What on earth are we going to say?'

Grandma put down the plate on the table and took hold of the back of one of the dining chairs with both hands. She leaned forward on the chair, her face thoughtful.

After a few seconds, she said. 'Your father just asked me if this is to do with the Sprite family magic.'

Flame groaned.

'It's all right,' said Grandma. 'In the circumstances, it's probably better that he knows. He is a Sprite, after all.'

Flame screwed up her face and shook her head. 'But what on earth are we going to say to Mum?'

Grandma turned to look at her. 'I think you – we – are going to have to be honest. The plan has been found out – and your mother will have a lot of questions. She might get a bit upset – so try to keep calm.'

Five minutes later, the family reconvened in the library. Everyone sat down as they had before. Grandma poured out fresh cups of tea and handed round glasses of juice to the girls.

In one hand, Mum held the plan. In the other, she held the letter.

'Right,' she said, holding up the letter. 'You say you found this letter behind Mim's portrait. Is that correct?'

The Sprite Sisters nodded.

'Then you started looking for the box, as the letter told you to?'

'Yes,' replied the girls.

'The letter says that when you found the box, you were *to*

guard the contents with your lives.'

'Yes,' the girls said again.

'Do you know *why* you had to guard it with your lives?'

Flame, Marina and Ash drew a breath and shook their heads.

Ariel stared at her hands. Then she piped up, 'I remember. Charles was looking for the box, too. We had to keep it safe from him.'

As she said this, her three sisters groaned.

'Here we go . . .' muttered Marina.

Mum gave a short laugh. *'Charles? Why was he looking for the box?'*

Ariel blinked. She heard her sisters murmur, 'No, Ariel!', but she was trying to remember. Why had Charles been looking for the box? Ah, yes, now she remembered.

Ariel blinked again. 'Glenda wanted it.'

'GLENDA?' gasped Mum. 'What's this got to do with *her?'*

'She wants the secret of the power, of course,' said Ariel. 'She told Charles to get her the box, as it held the plan.'

It was Mum's turn to blink.

'*What* power? What is all this stuff about "power"?'

Mum looked round at Dad. He was rubbing his chin, staring at the fire.

'Colin, do you understand this?' asked Mum.

Dad turned to look at her. He took a deep breath, then said in a quiet voice, 'Do you remember me telling you that magic power was supposed to run through the Sprite family?'

Mum raised her eyebrows in disbelief. 'Years ago – when we first met. I never took it seriously. Why?'

'Well, I think this is something to do with the magic,' said Dad.

Mum gave another short laugh. 'What, wizards and witches and all that nonsense?'

Dad nodded. 'Hm.'

'So, you're saying the girls have found some of the magic?'

Dad nodded again. 'Perhaps.'

'But I don't understand where Charles and Glenda fit in,' said Mum.

'Neither do I,' replied Dad.

Then Ariel blurted out, 'Well, Charles was bad at the beginning and he tried to use his dark power against us, because Glenda wanted to hurt us. But then he turned out to be good and when we got stuck in the portal he kept the door open, so we could get out. He saved our lives, so we like him now.'

Mum stared at Ariel with a look of horror. Her hand covered her open mouth, as she gave a gasp. Then she took her hand away – but still she could not speak. Silence filled the room. Then Dad looked across at Flame, then at Marina, then at Ash, then at Ariel. Lastly, he looked at his mother.

Then he said, 'How about you start at the beginning, please.'

Grandma looked calmly at her son and nodded. For a few seconds she was silent, collecting her thoughts. The Sprite Sisters waited. Dad sat back, a pensive look on his face.

Mum looked from daughter to daughter, to Dad and then to Grandma. Her face was pale and anxious – and had a hint of scepticism in its expression.

Then Grandma began.

First of all, she told Mum and Dad about the magic that ran through the Sprite family, and how some members had got it and others not. Of the Sprites who had it, she said, most had 'good' magic and were bound by the Sprite Code of Honour. But, she explained, another side of the family had turned towards 'dark' power.

'That was Margaret Sprite's side of the family,' she said.

'Wasn't she the ghost we had here at Hallowe'en?' asked Dad.

Grandma nodded. 'Yes – and she was Glenda Glass's grandmother.'

Dad listened carefully. Mum – who loved and respected her mother-in-law – tried to listen, but wondered if Marilyn's story was simply the ramblings of a mad, old woman.

It's all hocus-pocus, she thought to herself.

Grandma carried on. She talked about Sidney Sprite and how, when he had built Sprite Towers, he had embedded magic within the big house.

As she listened, Mum thought about how Ariel 'talked' to Sidney Sprite's portrait, which hung at the bottom of the stairs – and how Ariel claimed he 'talked' back to her. She looked across at Ariel, who was listening attentively to her grandmother.

Now Grandma was talking about her own magic power.

Mum said, 'Whoa!' and held up her hands. '*You* had magic power, Marilyn?'

Grandma nodded. 'Yes, dear.'

'*But you never told us!*'

'Sprites don't talk about their power – especially to people who don't have power.'

Mum's eyes widened. 'Why?'

'Because it would weaken it.'

Mum made a guffawing noise and looked round at Dad. He was watching his mother with wide eyes. '*You* have the magic power, Ma?'

'I did – but I lost my power a long time ago,' she said.

Mum looked at Grandma as if she were bonkers. She was about to speak when Dad put his hand out and said, 'Just listen, Ottalie – please.'

Mum sat back, exhaling loudly and shaking her head.

For the next half hour, Grandma told the story of how she had found she had magic power when she was nine years old. She had never told her parents because she thought they would not understand. Then, when she was a young ballerina, dancing in the *corps de ballet*, she found she had a rival. It turned out that this other dancer, Glenda, was also a Sprite. Glenda wanted to be the prima ballerina, but Marilyn was the better dancer.

Then she had met and fallen in love with Sheldon Sprite, Colin's father – and again, Glenda was jealous.

Glenda began to use a dark power against her, explained Grandma – to hurt her and get her out of the way. Grandma had fought back. Things spiralled and they had a big fight on a dark, empty street, late one night.

After that, Grandma had lost her power. 'It just disappeared from my hands,' she said, gazing at her long fingers.

'But why?' asked Mum.

'Because I'd used it to hurt someone,' explained Grandma. 'Good Sprites aren't allowed to do that.'

'But "bad" Sprites can?' said Mum, with an ironic smile.

Grandma ignored the jibe and nodded. 'Exactly.'

Mum raised her eyebrows and looked away.

As the flames crackled in the fire, the Sprite family was silent once more.

Then Mum said, 'So, Glenda wanted Sheldon. That would have changed things.'

'Yes – Colin might never have been born,' replied Grandma. She looked over at her son and said, 'But I think Glenda wanted Sprite Towers even more.'

Dad shook his head and smiled. 'Well, I never,' he said, quietly.

Mum crossed her arms in front of her and looked at Grandma. 'So, Marilyn – so how does this magic power actually work?'

'It comes out of our hands – it's like an energy, a force,' explained Grandma, holding out her hands. 'You feel it whooshing through your arm. You point your finger at something and you can change that thing in some way.'

Mum frowned. 'Change it – how?' Before Grandma could answer, she said, 'And what do you mean "*our*" hands?'

Everything went still. Then Mum said, 'Who else has this power?'

Grandma turned to look at the fire. Everybody waited. The only noise in the room was the sound of flames crackling.

Then Grandma turned to look at Flame. As she did this, Dad said, 'Flame?'

Mum looked at Dad, then at Flame, her face suddenly tense. *'What's this got to do with Flame?'*

Flame met her father's gaze. Keep calm, she thought. Grandma says be honest.

She drew herself up, her back straight. Then she looked across at her mother.

There she was, her mother, sitting on the sofa, with her curly blond hair and big grey eyes. But now her pretty smile had disappeared. Now her face was fearful.

Flame said quietly, 'Sit back, Mum, please – and just listen.'

Reluctantly, Mum sat back. As she did this, Dad put his arm across her shoulders and smiled at her.

Flame looked around at her sisters and her grandmother and drew in a deep breath. Then she said, 'Grandma was telling you how her magic power came to her when she was nine. Well, the same thing happened to me. I have a magic power, too.'

Mum shot forward on the sofa like a bullet. 'NO!' she cried. 'NO! I don't believe it!'

Flame stared at her, unsure what to say.

'It's all nonsense!' cried Mum, throwing up her arm. 'You're – you're a *normal* girl. You play the violin, you go to school and you work hard and – and you're – a – normal girl!'

Mum looked at Flame, her eyes angry now. Flame waited. Nobody spoke.

Dad sat forward and put his arm around Mum. 'Just listen, Ottalie, please.'

'But it's all NONSENSE!' spluttered Mum, gesticulating again.

Dad sighed heavily and looked across at Grandma, then at Flame.

Everybody waited.

Then Marina said, in a soft voice, 'It's not just Flame, Mum – it's all of us.'

Mum let out a muffled scream, her hand over her mouth – and stared at Marina in horror. '*You* too?'

Marina nodded.

Mum stood up, '*No, no – I won't listen any more. You're all talking nonsense!*' She stared down at her daughters. 'I've been a good mother! I've done the best I can to look after you. And I just want you to have normal lives!'

As she began to sob, Dad stood up beside her. 'Ottalie, please – sit down.'

On the sofa opposite, Ariel and Marina burst into tears. Ash looked at Flame with a sad face.

As Mum and Dad sat back down on the sofa, Flame gathered her thoughts.

'We are normal,' she said, her voice suddenly assertive. 'And you are a good mother – the best of mothers. But we do have the magic power of the Sprite family. *All four of us.*'

Mum looked across at her, sobbing.

Flame smiled. 'It's a wonderful thing to have a magic power, Mum! Really.'

'But it's dangerous,' said her mother, rubbing her hand across her face. 'You could get hurt.'

Flame looked at the fire. What her mother said was true. They had been hurt. They might have been killed. They might have been lost in the portal.

Then she said, 'The thing is, Mum – we don't have any choice.'

'But can't you just ignore it?' said Mum, wiping her face again.

'Well – we might have been able to . . .' said Flame.

'Except?'

'Except Glenda Glass kept trying to hurt us,' said Flame.

'*That woman again!*' spat Mum. 'What's the matter with her? Why does she want to hurt you?'

'Because she wants the secret of the power,' said Ash, leaning forward. 'And that's somehow connected to us and to Sprite Towers. That's why she moved here.'

Mum looked round at Ash, her face white. 'You're only ten!' she said, beginning to sob again. 'I don't believe this is happening!'

Then Marina sat forward. 'But listen, Mum! Our combined power is stronger than Glenda's – so we've been safe.'

Mum stared at Marina in horror and gave another sob.

For a while, they were silent again.

Dad stared at the fire, then looked across at his daughters. 'I'd like to know how your power works.'

Mum looked at him, sat back and dried her eyes.

Flame leaned forward. 'We have the powers of the four elements,' she explained. 'Mine is the power of Fire.'

Mum and Dad looked at one another. 'And we called you Flame?' they both said.

Flame laughed. 'Yeah, weird, isn't it?'

'And how does your power actually work?' asked Dad.

Flame looked across at Mum, wondering how she would

react. 'Well . . . well, I can burn things and light things up or melt them.'

Mum stared at her as if she were an alien.

Dad said, 'Just listen, Ottalie – don't say anything.' He looked across at Marina.

'I've got the power of Water,' she said, then waited as Mum and Dad exchanged more looks of surprise. 'I can create floods and rivers or suck out the fluid from something.'

Marina waited a few seconds, while Mum looked at her as if seeing her for the first time. Then she looked across at Dad and said, 'You remember when the roof was leaking in the summer?'

Dad nodded.

'Well, I used my power to suck out a lot of the water from the walls.'

Now it was Dad's turn to stare at his daughter as if she were an alien.

'And I work with the power of Earth,' said Ash, in her quiet voice.

'Strong like a tree and named after one,' said Dad, looking across at her with a soft smile.

Ash smiled back. 'My power allows me to sense where things are and to bind things down.'

Dad frowned. 'So, could you and Marina feel the water under the garden, when we had the flood just before Hallowe'en?'

'Yes,' replied Marina. 'And I knew that the ghost had escaped.'

Mum began to sob again, her face in her hands.

'Shh, Ottalie,' said Dad, gently.

He looked across at his youngest daughter. 'And you, Ariel?'

She sat forward and grinned. 'I work with the power of Air. I can lift things up. I lifted up Charles and stuck him to the ceiling!'

Mum gave a loud wail – and rushed out of the room.

That was the last the Sprite Sisters saw of their mother that evening. Ottalie Sprite was tough and rarely ill, but the news that her daughters had magic powers proved too much. Grandma followed her up to her bedroom, but Mum was too angry to talk to her. Angry that, for all these years, her mother-in-law knew something about her daughters that she did not know.

Grandma returned to the kitchen with a sad face. Dad had cooked supper and he and the girls were sitting round the table.

Several times, Flame's mobile had rung as Verena tried to reach her. In the uneasy silence, Flame ignored the calls. Although she was concerned about Verena, she could not face speaking to her.

They ate, silent and slightly mournful. And, when supper was cleared away, everyone went straight up to bed.

As Flame picked up the wooden box from the kitchen table, Dad said to her, 'I'd like to look at it, please.'

'But – but it has to be kept safe, Dad!'

'It will be safe with me,' he said, holding out his hand.

'But I've never let it go away from me,' said Flame,

her face suddenly anxious.

'I promise you I will look after the box,' said Dad.

'But Mum might . . .'

'The box will be safe with me,' he reiterated in a firm voice.

With that, Flame handed it over and went up to her room.

''Night, Sidney,' she said, as she passed the portrait of her great-great-grandfather at the bottom of the staircase. Family tradition held that everyone said goodnight to the normally smiling face of the founder of Sprite Towers as they went up to bed.

This evening even Sidney looks sad, thought Flame.

As the moon in its first quarter rose over the big, old house and a fox barked in the Wild Wood, the Sprite family settled into uneasy sleep.

CHAPTER TWELVE

ARGUMENTS AND CONFUSION

FLAME SHIVERED with cold as she drew back her bedroom curtains on Monday morning. The sky looked dark and ominous. Flurries of snow whirled around the big house.

Looks like we're in for some bad weather, she thought, gazing out of the window.

She turned and picked up her mobile. Several texts had arrived from Verena. Flame replied, saying they'd had a big upset the night before and that she hoped things were better at The Oaks.

Can I come over today? texted Verena.

Could be tricky, Flame texted back. *Mum is very upset about us having powers.*

The door opened and Ash came into the room. 'How did you sleep?' she asked.

Flame pushed her thick copper hair back from her face and grimaced. 'Same as you, by the look of it! Bit of a do last night.'

Ash stood beside her sister and looked out of the window. 'More snow coming,' she said, looking up at the sky.

'That's what I was just thinking,' said Flame.

A minute later, Marina and Ariel came in and flopped down on Flame's bed. Shivering, they pulled the red duvet over them. 'This house is *so* cold!' said Marina.

Flame and Ash sat down on the bed. The four sisters looked at one another with glum faces.

'Well?' asked Marina.

'I know you all think it's my fault,' said Ariel, pushing her ski-jump nose in the air.

'Why on earth did you have to tell Mum about Charles like that?' asked Flame. 'I can't believe you did that!'

Ariel sighed and rested her chin on her hands. 'I don't know why these things pop out like they do.'

'It's because you don't think before you speak!' said Flame, frowning.

'I *do* think!' said Ariel.

'Well, obviously not fast enough sometimes,' muttered Flame.

Ariel pursed her lips. 'Perhaps I was meant to say that.'

'Yeah, right,' said Flame. 'Good excuse.'

'How do you mean, Ariel?' asked Ash.

Ariel shrugged. 'Well – maybe Mum *has* to hear about

125

this. Maybe it's all part of the plan thingummyjig.'

Marina nodded. 'Could be. You mean it's as if everything has to come out in the open now – like with Verena.'

Ariel nodded.

'That makes sense,' agreed Ash.

'I've never seen Mum so upset before,' said Marina. 'It was awful.'

'She was completely freaked out,' said Ash.

They all looked down at the duvet, their faces sad.

'Mum's frightened,' said Flame. Things like this are not part of her world – so she tries to reason that they don't exist at all.'

'Most people are like that,' said Marina, with a wry smile. 'How many times do you hear people saying that rational human beings don't believe in ghosts and magic!'

Flame nodded. 'That's one of the main reasons we have to hide our power. Do you remember – Grandma told us it would frighten people.'

Ash screwed up her nose. 'Well, it's hardly surprising. I mean – it is all pretty weird, don't you think?'

Marina ruffled Ash's tufty hair and laughed. Flame and Ariel grinned.

'Well, I can't see that we'll ever convince Mum,' said Flame. 'And she was pretty cross with Grandma, so Grandma told me. She felt we'd all been hiding something from her.'

'Well – we have,' said Ash.

'For good reason,' Marina replied.

'Dad seemed cool about it, though,' murmured Ariel.

'Yes, he was, wasn't he,' agreed Flame. 'Maybe he is

remembering his Sprite roots.'

'Funny to think of Dad as a Sprite like that,' said Ash.

'He doesn't seem to be as frightened by the idea of us having magic power as Mum is,' said Marina.

Flame sighed. 'I don't know how we stop Mum worrying.'

'She's bound to worry – that's what mothers do,' said Marina. 'She loves us and she wants to keep us safe from harm.'

'She'd have a fit if she knew the half of it,' said Flame, shaking her head.

'Will we lose our magic power now that Mum knows?' asked Ariel.

Marina and Ash looked at her with anxious faces.

Flame looked thoughtful. 'Mum hasn't actually seen us use our power – and I think that's what counts.' As if to reassure herself, she held out her right hand and extended her index finger.

'It feels tingly,' she said. 'My power's still there.'

'Thank heavens for that,' murmured Marina. She looked down at her hands. 'I can feel my power there too,' she said.

'That's good, but how do we get round all this?' asked Ash.

'With great care,' said Flame, still looking at her finger.

Ariel looked up, as if suddenly woken from a dream. 'Has the plan changed again?' she asked.

'I'll check,' said Flame, getting up and moving towards the bookshelf. Then she stopped in her tracks and turned back to them. 'Blast! Of course – it's not here! Dad took the magic box from me last night – he said he wanted to look through it. He promised me he would look after it.'

'What?' said Marina and Ash, alarmed.

''Fraid I didn't have any choice,' said Flame. 'Dad demanded I hand it over.' She sat back and looked round at her sisters with a cross face. 'It's so annoying! We need it back. I want to know where the box is at all times.'

'And we can't see if the plan is changing if we haven't got it,' agreed Marina.

'Exactly,' said Flame, crossing her arms. She was silent for a few seconds, then said, 'Trouble is, I don't want to make a fuss in case Mum decides to hang on to it.'

'Good point,' agreed Marina.

'I'll ask him quietly as soon as I can,' said Flame. She looked at her sisters. 'Come on, we'd better get dressed and have some breakfast.'

'Yes, before we freeze to death up here,' said Marina.

'It's not that bad!' said Ash, as they raced out of the room.

The air crackled with tension at the breakfast table that morning. The Sprite family ate quietly. Everyone was polite – but none of them felt like speaking.

We're walking on eggshells, thought Flame, as she looked around the table.

Grandma caught her eye and gave her a quick smile, but her face was worried and drawn.

Flame looked across at Mum. Her face looked tired and lined. There was a sense of sadness in her, a heaviness in her mood, that Flame had never seen before.

There's a definite sense of unease between Mum and Grandma, she thought. Looks as if Mum is still upset with

Grandma for not telling her about our magic.

Dad looks tired, too, though more cheery, she thought. And my sisters look anxious.

The silence was not to last.

It was not in Ottalie Sprite's nature to bottle things up. Half French and a passionate woman who spoke her mind, it was not long before her fear about her daughters' safety surfaced again.

'I've been thinking about what you told us last night,' she announced suddenly. 'And I want you to promise me you won't use this magic power any more.'

Knives and forks clattered to the table as the Sprite Sisters gaped at their mother in complete disbelief.

'*No!*' shouted Flame. 'You can't do that!'

'But Mum, it's not for you to decide!' cried Marina.

Mum rounded on her second daughter with angry eyes. 'What do you mean, it's not up to me to decide? I'm your mother, for heaven's sake! If your father and I think something is not right for you, you will do as we say!'

Colin Sprite stared at his wife. 'But *Ottalie*!'

Mum spun round to him. 'You must agree, Colin! It's for their own sake – for their safety!'

'But we don't even know what's happened to them yet!' spluttered Dad.

'You don't understand, Mum!' shouted Flame, her face reddening. 'If we don't use our power to protect ourselves and Sprite Towers, we will lose the house and we *will* get hurt!'

'It's all absolute *nonsense* – all this magic power mumbo-jumbo!' said Mum, throwing down her napkin on the table.

'I don't believe a word of it!'

There was complete silence. Even little Archie stood still under the table.

Mum looked round at her daughters and waited. Nobody spoke.

Then Flame said, 'If you don't believe a word of it, why are you telling us we must not use our magic?'

Mum glared at Flame. Then she said, 'Okay – then prove it. Show me how you use your power and maybe I will believe you.'

'*No!*' the Sprite Sisters cried, together.

'We can't do that, Mum!' cried Ash.

'Why not?'

'*Because we'd lose our powers!*' replied Ash, her face white, her eyes wide.

'As far as I'm concerned that would be a good thing!' said Mum.

Flame looked at her mother with a defiant face. 'I'm not going to prove anything to you,' she said.

'You'll do as I tell you, young lady!' said Mum, standing up.

Flame stood up too. 'No, Mum – not this time,' she said, looking her mother in the eye. 'You don't understand what this all means.'

'THAT'S ENOUGH!' shouted Dad, banging his hand down on the table.

Everybody jumped with surprise.

'All right, calm down, everybody!' said Dad, in a stern voice.

Mum sat back down in her chair, followed by Flame. Little Archie crept to his basket. Ariel began to cry. Grandma held her forehead in her hand and sighed.

Dad looked round at them, one by one. 'Now – we are going to talk about this calmly and listen to each other.'

Mum put her elbows on the table, leaned her head on her fists and stared down.

Dad looked across at his eldest daughter. 'Flame, please would you go up to our bedroom and bring down the wooden box. It's on the carpet under my little bedside table. I'd like you all to explain how you use the secret plan and see if we can sort this out, somehow.'

As Flame dashed out of the kitchen, Dad touched Mum's arm and said, 'You've got to keep an open mind, Ottalie. There is a lot more to this than we realise – and it won't help if we don't listen.'

Mum made a face which seemed to suggest she doubted this, but said, 'Very well, then.'

They waited, silent. Flame's footsteps were suddenly audible, as she ran through the hallway and into the kitchen.

'Well?' said Dad, seeing Flame's empty hands and ashen-white face.

'*It's not there, Dad!*'

'What do you mean it's not there? It was there just before I came down to breakfast!' Dad looked round at Mum. 'Ottalie – have you put the box somewhere?'

Mum shook her head. 'No, I haven't touched it,' she said.

'Ma?' he said, looking at Grandma.

'No, dear,' she shook her head.

'It's gone, Dad!' cried Flame. 'You promised me you'd look after it – and it's *gone*!'

'Well, I don't know what's happened,' he said, getting up from the table. 'Let's go up and have a look.'

Grandma, Mum and Dad followed the Sprite Sisters as they raced up the stairs to the first floor and along the corridor. Mum and Dad's room was big and airy with a high ceiling, cream walls and a mushroom-coloured carpet. Long taupe curtains hung at the tall windows. Silver-framed family photographs sat on the top of two elegant wooden chests.

On either side of the big bed were two small tables, each with a lamp and a pile of books.

The Sprite Sisters kneeled down on the carpet and looked under Dad's bedside table. 'It's not here, Dad,' they said, then sat back on their heels.

Dad scratched his head. 'Well, I'm absolutely mystified. I saw it there only half an hour ago.'

Mum looked around the room, distractedly.

'Did you take it, Mum?' asked Flame.

Mum looked round. 'No – I told you I hadn't touched it,' she said, stung by Flame's accusing tone.

'That's enough, Flame,' said Dad.

Flame waved her arms and gave a roar. '*But where is it?*'

Before Dad could stop her, Flame launched into a tirade about the plan – how the sisters were supposed to guard it with their lives, how carefully they had kept it away from Glenda Glass and how they may never find it again.

'Then what, Dad?' she cried.

'Flame, stop it!' shouted Mum. 'That's enough!'

'I should never have given you the box, Dad,' sobbed Flame.

Mum and Dad looked round: all four daughters were crying. Grandma had her arms wrapped around the two younger girls. She gave Mum and Dad a steady look.

Ariel snuffled, then said in a mournful voice, 'It's gone into the portal and we'll never find it.'

At the word 'portal', Mum bristled. 'I doubt it,' she said in a crisp voice. 'Portals only exist in films.'

Ariel began to sob again.

Through her tears, Ash snuffled, 'Maybe George has taken it back.'

Dad began to search round the room. 'It's very strange,' he said. He looked over at Mum and said, 'Well, Ottalie, if you haven't taken it and I haven't taken it and Ma hasn't taken it – and none of the girls have, where do you think it's gone?'

'Are we sure the girls haven't got it?' asked Mum.

Dad looked at her with an expression of disbelief. The sisters all burst into more tears.

'I think we can assume that the girls have not got the plan, don't you?' said Dad in a low voice.

'Yes,' replied Mum, quietly.

Dad put his hands on his hips and gave a long sigh. 'So, what do we do?'

Grandma gave a little cough. Everyone looked round at her.

'The box that has disappeared is a magic box,' she said in

a clear voice. 'I expect it has magicked itself away. All we can do is trust it comes back.'

As she said this, Ash felt the magic stone in her pocket vibrate. She pulled it out and held it up on her open hand. A bright blue light shone out from the stone.

'What's that?' said Mum, with a look of surprise.

Ash held out the stone. It was round in shape, with two smooth, flattened sides and grey-brown in colour. Mum stared at it.

'It's my magic stone,' explained Ash. 'When it vibrates or lights up, it's telling me something.'

Mum gave a sharp laugh. 'What's it telling you now, then?'

Ash looked at the stone. 'Well, it vibrated when Grandma said it's "a magic box". So I guess it's telling us sisters not to worry.'

As she said this, the magic stone emitted a blast of bright blue light.

Mum jumped back in surprise.

'Wow!' giggled Ariel.

Dad laughed and shook his head. 'This gets more and more strange.' He looked over at Mum and said, 'How do you explain that?'

She bit her lip and shrugged.

'Wasn't that the stone that Charles found – the one you lost in the summer?' said Dad, as he peered down at it.

Ash nodded. 'Except that Charles didn't find it. He stole it from me. Ariel used her magic to trick him into giving it back to me.'

Dad looked at her with a shocked face. 'Oh,' he said, quietly.

'Here we go about Charles again,' said Mum. 'I think we should all go down and talk about this some more. I want to hear where Charles fits into this whole story.'

'I ought to go into the office, Ottalie,' said Dad. 'It's a busy time just now before Christmas.'

'Not this morning, Colin, please,' said Mum. 'We need to get to the bottom of this.'

CHAPTER THIRTEEN

THINGS GET WORSE

GLENDA GLASS stared at the Christmas tree standing in the hallway at The Oaks. The fairy lights twinkled; the baubles sparkled. Spread out on the ground under the tall tree were presents of all shapes and sizes wrapped in colourful paper and tied round with bows.

It all looks bright and happy, thought Glenda.

She sighed. Christmas. I've never worried about it before, but this year everything feels different, she thought. Why does it feel as if Christmas matters?

She turned and looked around the empty hallway and up the wide staircase: still no sign of Verena. She must be in her bedroom, thought Glenda.

Only a week now till Stephen gets back – and Zoe. Life

will change then. I shall go back to France and hardly ever see them.

I must go outside, she thought, suddenly feeling the need for fresh air.

A few minutes later, dressed for the cold weather, Glenda walked out of the front door and over the wide lawn towards the woods.

Up in her bedroom, Verena looked out of the window. What is Grandma doing, she wondered. It's freezing out there today.

She pressed her nose against the glass and watched her grandmother walk amongst the bare trees and swirling snowflakes. A wave of sadness washed over her.

Grandma looks so lonely, she thought.

That feeling was immediately followed by a wave of anger. It's not surprising if she does feel lonely, thought Verena. Grandma's only got herself to blame. She's a cruel, wicked woman . . .

But why is she walking round the garden? Something is different about her . . .

Verena turned to look at her room. I'm fed up being up here, she thought. I want to see the Sprites – but they're all having a big talk and I can't go over today.

Then a thought struck her. Perhaps I should talk to Grandma?

She turned again to look out of the window. Glenda was standing under a tree, looking down at the ground. Snowflakes whirled around her under the heavy, grey sky.

She looks so alone, thought Verena.

She walked out of her bedroom and down the stairs. In the kitchen, she turned on the kettle. By the time Glenda walked back into the house, Verena had prepared freshly ground coffee and a plate of biscuits.

'I've made us some coffee,' she said, holding the coffee things on a tray.

Glenda looked at her granddaughter with astonishment. 'Oh – that's very nice of you,' she said, taking off her coat and hat.

A minute later, they sat together in the sitting room, Glenda on the sofa and Verena in the armchair beside it. Verena poured the coffee and handed a cup to her grandmother.

Glenda's face was grey and drawn.

'You look tired, Grandma,' said Verena.

Glenda nodded. 'Yes,' she said, quietly. 'I have a lot on my mind and . . . I am . . . beginning to feel my age.'

Verena sipped her coffee thoughtfully, wondering whether to tell her grandmother about the Sprites. Normally the mention of the family had her seething. But some instinct told her it was time to be open. No more secrets, she thought. 'I had a text from Flame Sprite this morning.'

Glenda looked over at her. 'Oh?'

Relieved at this reaction, Verena continued. 'Yes, it seems that Colin and Ottalie have found out about their daughters' magic powers,' she said.

'*What?*'

'Apparently Ottalie hit the roof – and she's forbidden the girls to use their magic again.'

Glenda raised her eyebrows. 'Oh dear,' she said.

'Yes – oh dear.'

They were silent for a few seconds. Then Verena looked across at her grandmother and said, 'I wonder what Daddy and Mummy would do if they knew we had magic powers?'

Glenda's cold blue eyes for once looked uncertain. She shook her head. 'All my life, I never worried what anybody thought about me. I just did what I wanted, when I wanted – and life fell into place. Now, though . . .'

Verena waited, but Glenda was silent.

'What has changed?' she asked.

Glenda gave a long sigh. 'I think I have realised I have feelings.'

'Feelings?' asked Verena, with a frown.

'Hm.' Glenda nodded.

'What – like you mean you *care* about people?'

'Hm,' Glenda said again, looking across the room. 'And I am beginning to feel very alone.'

'Well, I suppose if you're not a nice person you will be alone, as people won't want to be with you,' said Verena.

Glenda looked round at her granddaughter and smiled an ironic smile.

'Well, it's true,' said Verena. 'We all want to be close to people we love and trust – and you haven't been very nice to people.'

Glenda stared across the room, a thoughtful look on her face.

For a while they were silent, each sipping their coffee and eating their biscuits.

Then Verena said, 'It feels like things are going to change.'

Glenda sighed. 'I think they already are.'

'Well, that's good, isn't it?' said Verena.

Glenda stared across the room, her eyes troubled. 'I suppose it depends how things change.'

Verena looked at her grandmother and waited. Then she said, 'Well – you know where to start, Grandma.'

Glenda looked round, meeting her granddaughter's clear blue eyes. Yes, she thought. I know where to start.

At Sprite Towers, the family sat round the kitchen table.

Mum's face was strained and tense. Dad's expression was one of concern. The Sprite Sisters looked anxious. Grandma looked tired.

'I don't know what to think,' said Mum, rubbing her hand across her forehead.

'I do know, though, that I'm not happy about any of this.' She looked around at her daughters and said, 'I'd like you to start from the beginning, again, and explain everything that has happened.'

Flame and her sisters looked across at one another, their hearts sinking.

'I'm not going to stop you this time,' said Mum. 'I'm going to listen – and I want the full story. As I'm sure your father does, too.'

Colin Sprite nodded.

Flame and her sisters had explained how they each came to their power when they were nine years old; how Glenda had first attacked them at the school concert in June – and how they had used the Circle of Power to defend themselves.

Mum and Dad remembered the concert and how Ash's cello string had suddenly broken and cut her face.

'And you're saying that Glenda caused the string to snap?' asked Mum, bewildered.

'Yes,' replied Flame. 'All the time we were playing, she was hurling her dark power at us.'

Mum blinked. 'It doesn't seem possible,' she said, quietly. 'Surely someone would have noticed if she was hurling "power" at you.'

The Sprite Sisters shook their heads.

'No, Mum,' said Marina. 'That's the point. Only people with magic powers would know what was really going on. Since you and Dad don't have them, you didn't see any more than anyone else sitting there.'

Mum looked at Grandma. 'Did you see what was happening, Marilyn?' she asked.

'Yes, I did – but I was powerless to help, I'm afraid,' she replied. 'The girls did well to repel Glenda's attack and play so well.'

'So this Circle of Power is what, exactly?' asked Dad.

Flame explained how the girls stood in a circle in the position of the four directions – east, south, west and north – and focused their power towards the centre of the circle.

'When we work together and balance our powers like this, we create a beautiful, blue light,' explained Flame. 'This light forms a big protective shield around us, that even Glenda's power can't penetrate.'

Mum and Dad stared at Flame, then looked at one another

with a look of amazement.

Then Dad rubbed his hand across his forehead and said, 'So – you're saying that when you do this, you four girls are more powerful than Glenda.'

'Yes,' replied Flame.

'But you'd be vulnerable if you were alone.'

Flame nodded. 'Yes, I think we might be.'

Dad frowned.

It was when Flame started to explain how Glenda attacked Sprite Towers that Mum began to cry. Everybody waited, nervously, as Marina got up and brought her a box of tissues.

Grabbing a handful, Mum said with a muffled sob, 'Carry on.'

'So, was that when the water came through the roof?' asked Dad.

'Yes,' replied Flame. 'Glenda used her dark power to create the holes in the roof and the water – so that the roof would fall in. She knew we didn't have enough money to repair it – and that would force you to sell Sprite Towers.'

'Water was pouring in all over the roof,' remembered Dad. 'It felt like the house was under siege.'

'We *were*, literally,' said Flame. 'Glenda was determined to get Sprite Towers.'

'That woman is evil personified,' said Mum. 'She seems to stop at nothing.'

'Thankfully, Mrs Duggery came to help us,' said Ash.

'Mrs Duggery?' said Mum, wiping her eyes. 'Mrs Duggery has magic power, too?'

'She's a Sprite with special magic powers, Mum,' said Ash.

'But she's absolutely ancient!' said Mum, aghast.

'Violet Duggery is Sidney Sprite's niece,' said Grandma. 'She is *very* old – but she is the most powerful Sprite of all.'

Mum stared at Grandma as if she was bonkers.

'Grandma's right, Mum – Mrs Duggery has incredibly strong magic power,' said Ash.

Then Marina broke in. 'You don't know it, but Glenda attacked the house when you and Dad went away for the weekend. There was a terrible wind and noise and everything was shaking. Grandma thought the towers would fall. Glenda was outside on the lawn, sending her dark power towards the house.'

Mum stared at Marina, her mouth open.

'It was absolutely terrifying,' said Ariel.

'We managed to stop Glenda using our magic powers – but it left the house and grounds in the most terrible state,' said Flame.

'And Grandma was badly hurt,' added Ariel.

Dad looked round at Grandma. 'You didn't tell us you'd been hurt, Ma.'

Grandma smiled and shrugged. 'I was okay. Just had a nasty hit on the head.'

'You were knocked out cold, Grandma!' said Ariel. 'I thought you were dead.'

'Marilyn!' cried Mum. 'This is dreadful!' Grabbing another handful of tissues, she began to cry again.

Grandma got up to put on the kettle. Everybody was silent. Marina bent down to stroke Archie, who was wandering around under the table.

'So then what happened?' asked Dad.

'My rabbit, Fudge, was killed by a falling branch,' said Ash.

'Oh, Ash – I'm so sorry,' said Dad. 'I remember you'd just buried him when we got home.'

'The house was all broken and there was the most terrible mess,' said Flame. 'But with Mrs Duggery's help, we managed to clear everything up just before you arrived back.'

'Mrs Duggery was amazing!' said Marina, waving her hands. 'She went *whoosh* and things were mended!'

Ariel looked round at her sisters and giggled. 'Do you remember how she walked along the top of the roof, way up in the air, carrying that enormous pile of tiles?'

Her sisters laughed.

Dad peered at Ariel. 'Hang on a minute,' he said. 'You say Mrs Duggery was on the *roof*?'

'Yes,' said Ariel.

'When was that?'

'On Sunday afternoon, just before you and Mum got back,' giggled Ariel.

Dad looked round at Mum. 'I *told* you I saw Mrs Duggery on the roof as we drove up the drive!' he said, incredulous. 'You didn't believe me!'

'Well, it's hardly surprising, Colin!' she said. 'This is all so awful.'

Dad put his arm round her shoulders. 'Come on, love,' he said, softly.

'Well, I don't know how you can sit there and listen to this so calmly!' she cried. 'It's all – all – so – *unreal*! And the girls and your mother have been in so much danger!'

144

Dad exhaled hard and waited until Mum calmed down. Then he looked across at his daughters and asked, 'So what happened after that?'

'The next thing was when Charles came,' replied Ash.

As Grandma brought fresh coffee and drinks for the girls, the Sprite Sisters explained how Charles had been working for Glenda, as well as doing the art inventory on the house.

The thought that someone had been in the house that they could not trust *really* upset Mum. For the next few minutes, they were all quiet as she cried. Then she dried her eyes and said, 'Carry on with the story.'

The Sprite Sisters explained how Charles had been looking for the magic box, but that they had found it first.

'Once we found the plan in the box, we knew we had to use it – but we didn't know what we would find,' explained Flame.

'It turned out we created a portal – a doorway to go back in Sprite family time,' explained Marina.

Mum and Dad looked absolutely flabbergasted. 'Oh!' Mum cried, holding her tissues in front of her mouth.

Everyone was silent.

Then Dad said, in a very quiet voice, 'So what happened?'

The Sprite Sisters looked at one another, uncertain whether to explain what happened next.

Dad waited, watching them. Mum was sobbing quietly.

'Well, Ariel stood a bit close – and Charles did, too,' said Flame. 'And they both fell into the portal.'

'But George Sprite brought them out,' added Marina, very quickly.

'George Sprite?' asked Dad.

'Yes, the young man who died on the Front – the one who wrote us the letter,' said Ash.

Dad rubbed his forehead hard and stared down at the table.

Mum sobbed loudly. 'Ariel might have been lost for ever!'

Which, of course, was true. For a long while, the family sat at the table silent, their hearts heavy.

Then Dad said, 'What happened after that?'

Flame looked across at him. 'The last thing was the ghost at Hallowe'en.'

Mum dried her eyes and looked at Flame with a weary face.

'Now, *this* you know about, Ottalie,' said Dad. 'You remember how you felt something icy cold go past you that morning the engineers drilled the bore hole in the lawn?'

'Yes,' she snuffled. 'I remember that.'

'And how the lights went out when Verena came?' said Flame.

'And how cold it was when the ghost was around?' added Ash.

'Yes,' replied Mum. She remembered those things, too.

Drawing a deep breath, Flame explained how she worked out that they had to go into the portal, to meet with Margaret Sprite. 'I realised the only way to get Margaret out of Sprite Towers was to change the way she felt about her brother, Sidney,' she said. 'She was driven by jealousy and a sense of injustice – just like Glenda has been. I knew I had to show Margaret this photograph I had found.'

Mum and Dad exchanged worried glances, as Marina and

Ash explained how the girls opened the portal and went in.

'We went back in time and we met with Margaret,' explained Marina. 'She was really nasty, but when Flame showed her a photograph of her and Sidney when they were children, it made her remember how they loved each other. It took away the bad feeling and the bitterness.'

'So she didn't want to hurt us – and she wouldn't help Glenda hurt us, either,' added Ash.

'But we did have a job getting out of the portal,' said Flame, quietly. 'We'd left it late to return and the door nearly closed on us. We have Charles to thank for keeping it open.'

At this Mum cried out in horror. Dad looked really upset, too. He put his arm around Mum.

'Charles saved us, Mum,' said Ariel.

'He's become a "good" Sprite,' said Ash. 'He doesn't work for Glenda any more – so we can trust him.'

Mum put her face in her hands and sobbed. Everyone else sat silent for a while. None of them had ever seen Mum so upset before.

Ariel gripped her grandmother's hand. Ash and Marina exchanged sorrowful looks.

Flame was concentrating on the story. 'And Mrs Duggery – she saved us, too,' she said.

Dad screwed up his face. 'Hang on a minute. Was that the morning when I came down early to let out the dogs and Charles and Mrs Duggery were sitting in the kitchen drinking coffee, as if they'd been there for hours?'

'Yes,' said Flame, with a smile. 'They gave you a bit of a shock.'

Dad shook his head. 'I'll say so. I never found out how they got in – was sure I'd locked the door.'

'A locked door won't stop Mrs Duggery,' giggled Ariel. 'She can get through anything.'

Mum blew her nose loudly, then she looked round at her daughters. Her face was swollen and puffy. She looked very distressed. Everybody waited as she dried her eyes. Then she drew herself up and said in a firm voice, 'Well, I have listened to your story and I stand by what I said to you all yesterday. I forbid you to use any more magic.'

Dad looked at his daughters, his face drawn and worried. They sat, staring down, their faces lost and empty

'Colin, you will support me in this!' said Mum. 'There can be no question of the danger the girls have been in. They must not use any more magic – ever.'

Dad was silent, rubbing his chin with his hand.

'COLIN!' said Mum, sharply.

'Yes, Ottalie, I *heard* you,' he replied, equally sharply.

There was silence. Then Mum looked at Grandma and said, her voice tense, her face angry, 'And I'm very upset that you've allowed this go on, Marilyn – and that you hadn't told us about the girls' magic.'

Grandma looked as if someone had slapped her in the face. Standing behind her, Marina and Ash looked across at their mother with angry eyes. Ariel sat in a heap.

Flame's face reddened. '*You haven't listened, Mum!*' she shouted across the table.

'*I have listened!*' shouted Mum, standing up and facing her eldest daughter.

'You may think you have listened, but you don't under-stand!' shouted Flame.

'How dare you speak to me like that!' Mum shouted back.

Dad jumped up and put his hands out. 'Okay, that's enough, everybody.'

Flame burst into tears. 'The point is, we don't choose the magic – it finds *us*. There is something we still have to do – something we have to complete in this house.'

'We have to find the treasure, Mum!' cried Ariel, looking up.

'*You are not to use any more magic!*' shouted Mum. 'NO MORE MAGIC! *Do you understand?*'

Silence filled the big kitchen.

Ariel burst into tears. 'Now we'll never find the treasure!'

'Well, since the plan has disappeared I doubt we'll be able to,' said Flame, with a sullen face.

Marina and Ash stood behind their grandmother, wiping their eyes.

'And I think you've been incredibly unkind to Grandma!' shouted Flame. 'You're blaming her for all this – and all she has done is help to protect us!'

And with that, she marched out of the kitchen and banged the door behind her.

Grandma got up from the table and said, her voice shaky, 'I think I'll go up to my room for a little while.' And she walked out, too.

Marina, Ash and Ariel followed.

Mum and Dad were left sitting alone in the kitchen, their faces pale with shock.

'I can't believe our children have been in so much

danger,' sobbed Mum. 'It's awful to think about what might have happened.'

Dad got up and walked to the window and stared out towards the bare trees. After a while he turned to Mum and said, 'I don't understand you, Ottalie. You seem to know the girls have been in danger, but you still don't really believe in magic power!'

Mum shook her head. 'I don't know what to think, Colin,' she said, in a quiet voice. 'This has challenged everything I have ever believed in. I have no experience of magic power. I don't see or hear things like the girls do, apparently. I just know I want our children to be safe.'

'You don't think that, even if you can't see or feel something, it might still exist?' Dad asked.

Mum sighed. 'Well, let's say I am more open to the idea.' She looked across at Dad. 'I suppose it all makes more sense to you, being a Sprite?'

He nodded. 'Perhaps it is that. I was shocked by a lot of what the girls said – and I worry that they were in danger. But there was a part of me that felt it was all *real*. I believed everything they told us. Weird, I know.'

He held out his hands and wiggled his fingers. 'I wonder what it would be like to feel magic power surging through your hands? Pretty amazing, I should think.'

Mum got up from the table, walked towards him and held his arm. 'I'm so sorry I upset your mother,' she said, gently.

Dad looked into her eyes. 'She was very hurt by what you said.'

'I know,' said Mum, meeting his gaze. 'I'll go up and

apologise to her. I know how much she loves the girls. I was angry and frightened – and I lashed out.'

'It's more than just loving the girls,' said Dad. 'Ma obviously understands the whole picture in a way that neither you nor I do. In the circumstances, the girls are lucky to have had her guidance. She's a wise woman, my mother, and she would never hurt her family.'

Mum sighed again. 'I know. I see that now.'

Together they stared out of the window at the swirling snow. Then Mum walked out of the kitchen and up to Grandma's room.

CHAPTER FOURTEEN

GRANDMA
PAYS A VISIT

THE REST of the day passed very quietly. Worn out by the long argument, the Sprite Sisters went to their rooms. In the kitchen, Mum and Grandma baked bread and prepared more food for Christmas. Dad went off to his office.

Supper that evening was the quietest meal any of them could remember. The Sprite Sisters sat with glum faces. Mum tried to make conversation, but none of her daughters responded more than they had to. Dad was unusually quiet, his face drawn. Grandma looked preoccupied.

After supper, when the girls were ready for bed, Grandma sat in Flame's room and talked to them.

'I understand why your mother is so upset,' she said. 'You must try and see it from her point of view. Mothers are protective creatures and she's frightened that something awful could happen to you.'

'She was unkind to you,' said Ariel.

'And she has apologised,' said Grandma. 'I was upset, I know – but we have talked and we understand one another. I think your mother realises, now, that I have tried to guide you.'

'Dad seems to understand it all much more than Mum,' said Ash.

Grandma smiled. 'He's a Sprite. Magic is in his bones. Perhaps that makes it easier for him to understand. Your mother has never had any time for anything magical. It's just not part of her thinking. Most people are like that.'

Flame nodded and sighed.

They were silent for a few seconds, then Flame said, 'What are we going to do about Glenda?'

'How do you mean?'

'Well, there's the money she's stolen from you for starters,' said Flame. 'We have to get that back. Then there's stopping her from hurting us any more.'

Grandma looked thoughtful.

Flame said suddenly, 'Funny thing is that when Verena called me this morning, she said Glenda was different.'

'Different?' asked Grandma.

'Hm – sort of preoccupied and quiet,' said Flame. 'And just much *nicer*.'

'*Nicer*? That's not the Glenda we know!'

They all laughed.

'Verena thinks her grandmother is lonely,' added Marina. 'She thinks Glenda doesn't want to have to leave

The Oaks once Zoe gets back next week.'

'And I think we already told you that Verena told her grandmother she has to return your money,' added Flame. 'She told Glenda that we all know and she said that seemed to worry her.'

'And she's told Glenda about Mum and Dad finding out about our powers and all that,' added Marina.

'It just goes to show that things don't stay hidden for ever,' said Grandma.

'So what about your money?' asked Flame. 'Have you a plan?'

Before Grandma could answer, Ariel said, 'Will Glenda go to prison?'

Grandma shook her head. 'I don't know, love.'

'It would serve her jolly well right,' said Ariel. 'Horrible woman! I hope she gets thrown into a deep dungeon and left to starve – with rats crawling all over her.'

They all shuddered. 'Urgh!' said Marina.

'Ariel's right, though – Glenda should be made to suffer,' said Ash.

Grandma nodded, her face serious. 'She's done immense damage,' she said. Then she looked across at Flame. 'I have been giving the matter of my money some thought.'

'But you're not going to tell us at the moment,' said Flame.

Grandma smiled. 'No, not just yet – but I promise I am thinking about it.'

Just then the door opened and Mum came in. She looked slightly awkward, as if she felt she was interrupting something.

'Bedtime,' said Grandma, standing up.

Five minutes later, Mum and Grandma walked back down the wide staircase.

'Flame was just asking me what I'm going to do about Glenda returning the money,' said Grandma.

'What did you say?'

'Well, I didn't tell them but I think the best thing is for me to confront Glenda – to go round and talk to her.'

Mum looked worried. 'But from what the girls say, she's dangerous. She could hurt you.'

'I know – and I've thought about that,' said Grandma. 'I just have to take a chance.'

'When will you go?'

'First thing in the morning,' said Grandma. 'But please don't tell the girls. I don't want Verena to warn Glenda that I'm coming over.'

'Take her by surprise, you mean,' said Mum. She sighed. 'Well, I shall be thinking of you, Marilyn – and I really hope you can get your money back.'

'I know you do, my dear,' smiled Grandma.

Tuesday morning was cloudy and cold. Marilyn Sprite wrapped up well before she got into her car and drove down the drive of Sprite Towers. At the road, she turned left along the narrow country lane towards The Oaks. The road was icy and she drove with care. Here and there across the fields was the odd smattering of snow.

A few minutes later, she pulled into the driveway and got out of the car.

Resolve, she said to herself as she walked towards the imposing front door. Grabbing the brass door ring, she drew a deep breath and knocked twice.

The door opened.

Glenda Glass stared with surprise. 'Marilyn Sprite,' she said, as their eyes met.

'Good morning, Glenda. I know it's early and we haven't arranged this, but I'd like to have a chat, please.'

Glenda hesitated. Then she opened the door wide and said, 'Come in.'

Marilyn entered the big hallway and looked at the Christmas tree. 'Is Verena here?'

Behind her, Glenda shut the door. 'She hasn't come down yet. Bit early for her.'

Glenda showed Marilyn Sprite into the drawing room and closed the door. The two women sat down: Marilyn on the cream silk sofa, Glenda on the armchair.

The two women looked remarkably alike: almost the same age, similar colouring, tall and slim, straight-backed with their dancer's posture and sharp noses. Marilyn's strawberry-blond hair had faded to a pale blond and was cut into a smart bob. Glenda's pale blond hair was pulled back into a chignon.

Marilyn's green eyes met Glenda's blue eyes.

'Well?' said Glenda.

'I expect you know why I am here.'

Glenda raised her eyebrows, as if to say, 'Do I?'

They were silent for a few seconds, then Marilyn said, 'As I've grown older, I've become increasingly conscious of the value of a loving family. Perhaps I feel more vulnerable with age and feel the need for a sense of protection. I'm very lucky to have my family around me – and that we all get on so well. There's a lot of love there, and for that, I am very grateful.'

Marilyn waited, wondering if Glenda would comment – perhaps admit some sense of change in her life – but she said nothing.

'Things seem to be coming out into the open,' continued Marilyn. 'First there's Verena's new magic power. Then, as she may have told you, Ottalie and Colin have found out about their daughters' magic powers.'

Glenda watched Marilyn, her face impassive.

Marilyn looked thoughtful. 'Colin understands the magic a little, I believe, but Ottalie is very unhappy about it all. It's caused a lot of upset and division.'

Glenda stared at Marilyn, surprised at her frankness. 'Is this what you came to tell me?' she asked.

'Partly,' said Marilyn. 'I wanted you to know that things are changing for all of us – and that things are no longer hidden as they once were. I believe it is time for all of us to be open.'

Glenda raised her eyebrows and nodded. 'And?' she said.

Resolve, thought Marilyn, as their eyes met again.

'And I believe you have something that is mine.'

Glenda's reaction was instant. Her eyes narrowed and her body stiffened. For a second, Marilyn wondered what would happen. But then Glenda looked down at her hands and said nothing.

After a few seconds, Marilyn said, 'It will save a lot of heartache and embarrassment to you and your family – and to mine – if you would return the money that I believe you have taken from me.'

She waited again. Glenda was silent, sat staring ahead.

'If it is returned to me before Christmas, I will not mention to Stephen and Zoe what has happened and the matter will be dropped,' said Marilyn, her voice getting more assured. 'Verena, I believe, knows about it already. However, if my money is not returned, then I will start criminal proceedings to get it back. I understand we have enough evidence now to make a case.'

She waited again. Glenda sat silent.

Marilyn Sprite sighed. Then she said in a quiet but firm voice, 'You have done much harm, Glenda – but, despite this, I would prefer that peace and harmony are restored to our families. If restitution is made, the matter will lie there. If you want to build a new life with your family, I recommend you put away your grievances and your dark power. Anger is a lonely road to travel. We're both getting older, and I hope a little wiser. Our two families have grown closer over the last six months – and there seems, at last, to be friendship growing between Verena and the girls. They are the new generation. They have powerful magic and they need to learn to use it wisely and for the good of all. They need guidance and love.'

Glenda turned. Her blue eyes met Marilyn's. Her expression remained impassive and still she was silent.

'Well, I've said my piece,' said Marilyn, with a small smile. 'The rest is up to you.'

She got up off the sofa and walked towards the door. Glenda sat as if frozen, watching her.

'I'll see myself out,' said Marilyn.

A minute later, she started the engine and pulled out of the driveway.

I told her, she thought, with a smile. I said it! All these years and all those terrible things – and it comes down to this. Give it back, or you risk losing the love and respect of your family.

Well, she thought. I'll just have to wait and see now. Six days till Stephen and Zoe get back on Christmas Eve. I wonder what Glenda will do?

As she drove home along the icy lane, Marilyn Sprite breathed a huge sigh of relief.

'Where have you been, Grandma?' asked Flame, as she walked back into the kitchen at Sprite Towers.

'I went to see an old acquaintance.'

'Who's that?' asked Flame.

Grandma smiled. 'Can't you guess?'

Flame screwed up her face. 'Glenda?'

'Hm.'

Flame's mouth fell open. 'Blimey! Did you feel safe?'

'Yes, I did. I think Verena may be right – that she has changed.'

'What did she say?'

'Very little – but I asked her for my money back before Christmas,' replied Grandma. 'Now we will have to wait and see.'

A faraway look passed over Flame's face. 'The plan is still missing,' she said. 'We're all waiting for things to happen.'

'Have you spoken to your mother this morning?' asked Grandma.

Flame shook her head. 'I've been speaking to her as little as possible. I feel really upset and so do the others. I think Mum took the plan and has hidden it away.'

Grandma frowned. 'She said she hadn't – and your mother is honest. She would not do that.'

'But she doesn't believe us about our magic – and it hurts.'

Grandma put her arm around Flame's shoulder. 'Well, I do, love. And I think your mother is hurting just as much, so don't be too hard on her.'

Apart from the prospect of their grandmother's money being returned and the impending return of Zoe and Stephen, the Sprite Sisters' mood was glum. They walked around with long faces and heavy hearts, feeling increasingly anxious about the disappearance of the secret plan and not being able to use their magic to find it.

Despite Mum's apology to Grandma and her efforts to keep the mood level, the Sprite Sisters felt very upset. How could she forbid them to use their magic power, they asked each other. Surely it was not up to her.

'I feel as if my hands have been cut off,' said Marina, holding them out and staring at them.

'That's a bit extreme,' said Flame, with a frown.

'It's sad to think I may never feel my magic whooshing

through my fingers again,' said Marina.

Flame exhaled heavily. 'Hm,' she agreed. 'But we don't *have* to do what Mum says . . .'

They sat silent for a moment, thinking on this.

Then Ash held out her magic stone on her palm. 'Mum hasn't asked me to give her my magic stone,' she said. 'I don't want to lose it.'

'No, Ash – you mustn't give it to her,' said Flame.

'Don't mention it and maybe Mum will forget you have it,' said Marina. 'And Ariel, don't you dare say anything!'

Ariel screwed up her mouth. 'You always blame me,' she said.

And so they went on, each feeling unhappy and frustrated.

All through Tuesday, the harder Mum tried to get her daughters to open up, the quieter they seemed to be – even Ariel, who was the closest to her. None of the girls were rude to her; there was simply a distance between them that had never been there before.

'It's as if the stuffing's been knocked out of them,' Mum commented to Dad that evening. 'They're all so lethargic – and they seem bored.'

'Well, the stuffing *has* been knocked out of them, if you think of this from their point of view,' replied Dad. 'I think they feel that part of them has been denied.'

'I only want to protect them,' said Mum, for the umpteenth time.

'I know – and I see both points of view,' said Dad.

'They're very distant towards me,' said Mum.

'I noticed.'

'I think they think I've secretly hidden the plan from them.'

Dad sighed again. 'I wonder where on earth that went? Well, let's hope things cheer up before Christmas. It's awfully gloomy here at the moment.'

'And let's hope that Marilyn is successful,' added Mum.

'Absolutely,' agreed Dad.

At The Oaks that night, Glenda Glass looked out of her bedroom window. Clouds scudded across the inky sky as the moon rose over the trees.

It looks cold and bleak out there, she thought. I am warm in here. I feel – safe . . .

What am I to do? What *can* I do?

In a matter of days, Stephen and Zoe will be home. What will they do when they learn the truth? Why do I *care*, all of a sudden?

She thought of Marilyn Sprite sitting on the sofa. She looked well. She looked content, she remembered.

Perhaps Marilyn is right: we are getting older and things have changed.

I used to be able to keep things hidden. All my life, I was able to keep things secret. Even my husbands did not know who or what I really was – or how I used them. If things got difficult, I would leave and start again. But not any more . . . I don't want to do that now . . .

The Sprite Sisters' magic has changed everything. I have been unable to beat them and now things are known about us all.

Too many people know now for me to just disappear.
So what shall I do about Marilyn's money?
What shall I *do*?

CHAPTER FIFTEEN

MRS DUGGERY ARRIVES

ON WEDNESDAY morning, the sky was clear and a sharp frost lay on the ground.

Around mid-morning, there was a rap on the front door. Flame went to open it.

'Mrs Duggery!' she exclaimed, seeing the tiny, wizened old lady standing on the doorstep. For a second, Flame was speechless with astonishment. Why was Mrs Duggery here? Then, remembering her manners, she opened the door. 'Come in!'

'Mornin',' said Mrs Duggery in her broad Norfolk accent. She clumped through the doorway in her big brown boots. On her head was the lilac knitted hat that she always seemed to wear. Today she also wore a thick tweedy coat, which she took off in the hallway. As Flame hung it up in the cupboard, Mrs Duggery looked around the hall.

'Like them leafy decorations,' she said, noticing the holly and ivy that Mum and the girls had woven in and out of the banister rails up the staircase and round the first floor landing. 'Tha's right pretty,' she said, approvingly.

'Yes, we think so,' agreed Flame. She looked at Mrs Duggery with a sudden sense of unease. Why is she here, she wondered. Has she come to tell us off about losing the plan? She's terrifying when she's in a good mood, thought Flame. Gawd knows what she'd be like if she was angry . . .

'Soon be Christmas,' said Mrs Duggery, still admiring the decorations. 'Right, then, let's get on.'

Flame opened the door into the kitchen and said, 'Look who's come to see us!'

As Mrs Duggery stomped in, Mum and Grandma, Marina, Ash and Ariel came forward, smiling.

Bert toddled up, wagging his tail. Archie bounced around Mrs Duggery's feet and tried to chew one of her bootlaces.

'Violet, how nice to see you!' said Grandma, giving her a hug.

'Mrs Duggery, come in, and welcome,' said Mum. 'I'll make some coffee.'

'Hello!' said Marina and Ash, with big smiles.

'Are you going to tell us off about the missing plan?' asked Ariel, standing in front of the tiny old lady. There was little difference in height between them. 'The box disappeared, you know, and we have no idea where it's gone. And we're *very* worried.'

As Mum prepared the coffee in the kitchen, Mrs Duggery watched the youngest Sprite Sister with her dark glinty eyes.

Ariel rattled on, 'And Mum and Dad know about our magic powers and Mum has said we mustn't use our magic *ever* again – and we're very upset about that, too. It's been an *awful* week.'

'Tha' dunt sound too good,' agreed Mrs Duggery.

'So we haven't found the treasure yet,' said Ariel, with a big sigh.

'No well nor you wunt, if yer han't got the plan,' said Mrs Duggery.

'We don't know where it's gone,' said Ash. 'It vanished from under Dad's bedside table.'

Mrs Duggery looked up at Flame.

'It's my fault,' said Flame, with a frown. 'I should never have taken it out of my bedroom and shown it to Dad.'

'It's not your fault,' said Marina. She looked at Mrs Duggery. 'Dad asked to see the magic box, so Flame had to go and get it. He and Mum wanted to know all about our magic powers. It's been terrible.'

Mrs Duggery nodded, her eyes still glinting.

Ariel looked at Mrs Duggery with a serious face. 'George Sprite told us to guard it with our lives and we kept it safe from Glenda and Charles – and now it's just – just – *gone*!'

Mum now stood beside them holding a tray of coffee and chocolate biscuits. 'We're ready,' she said. 'How did you get here, Mrs Duggery?'

Mrs Duggery fixed the biscuits with her sharp eyes and

replied, 'On me bike, same as always.'

'The roads are very icy,' said Mum.

'Yep,' agreed Mrs Duggery, still looking at the biscuits.

Mum was about to tell everyone to go through to the library, when Mrs Duggery said, 'Ottalie, I wonder if I could have a word with you an' Marilyn.'

'Of course,' said Mum, slightly surprised. 'Girls, have your drinks and a biscuit here. We'll go through.'

The Sprite Sisters exchanged anxious glances as Mum, Grandma and Mrs Duggery walked out of the kitchen.

'Oh no,' groaned Ash.

'It's all my fault,' said Flame, shaking her head.

'It's not your fault,' said Marina.

A few minutes later, Mum, Grandma and Mrs Duggery sat by the library fire. Mrs Duggery sat on one sofa. Mum and Grandma sat opposite on the other. In between them was the low table with the tray.

Mrs Duggery was munching her fourth chocolate biscuit when she looked straight at Mum and said, 'Now wa's this I heard about yer not lettin' the girls use their magic?'

Mum drew a quick breath. 'Well . . .' she hesitated. 'I don't want my daughters to be in danger.'

Mrs Duggery nodded. 'I understan'.'

Mum relaxed a little.

Mrs Duggery was silent for a few seconds. Then she said, 'So, what would you tell them ter do if Glenda Glass used her dark power on 'em? Would you tell 'em ter just stand there an' get hurt? Or would you want 'em ter defend themselves?'

Mum looked worried at this thought. 'Couldn't they avoid Glenda?'

Mrs Duggery gave a sharp laugh, her dark eyes still fixed on Mum. 'Glenda were owt ter get em and she could've hurt 'em right bad. And yer house! No, she wouldn't let 'em avoid her.'

Mum looked away and sighed a big sigh, then she looked back at Mrs Duggery. 'I don't know. This – this whole thing about magic frightens me. I don't understand it – I'm not sure I even believe any of it. I certainly don't want anyone to get hurt.'

'Yes, I know, my dear – thas hard fer you,' said Mrs Duggery. 'But thas *owt there*. If magic power finds yer owt, yer *hav* ter deal with it. Yer can't walk away from it. That int how it works.'

Mrs Duggery leaned forward and took another biscuit. 'Mos' people will never know about these things – they think it jus' happens in books. But, like it or not, your girls are Sprites. Magic is a part a' their lives now – an' it always will be. There int nothin' you can do about it.'

Mum was about to say something, but Mrs Duggery put up her hand. 'Ottalie, my dear, all that these girls have told yer over the last few days – and Marilyn, here – *thas all true*. You stop 'em using their magic and a part on 'em will dry up and wither. Yer hav ter trust 'em. Yer mother-in-law has guided 'em well. An' I bin lookin' on.'

Mum bristled. 'How do you know what we've been saying? How do you know what happens here when you're not here?'

Mrs Duggery's eyes glinted. 'I jus' know. Thas part'a my

magic. I know everything tha' go on here.'

Mum looked aghast. 'You're a very strange lady, Mrs Duggery.'

Mrs Duggery laughed. 'That I am!' she agreed, to which Mum gave a small, uncertain smile.

Then Mrs Duggery fixed Mum with her dark eyes and said, 'Now, my dear, there's some important magic we have ter do. Some healing magic ter set the family straight.'

Mum tensed. 'But —'

'No buts, Ottalie. This is fer *all* the family. All the Sprites – right the way across ter Glenda and Verena.'

Mum blinked. 'Glenda?'

Mrs Duggery nodded. 'An' once we got tha' all dun, yer daughters'll be much safer an' everyone'll be a lot happier.'

Mum looked round at Grandma for reassurance.

'Please listen to what Mrs Duggery has to say,' said Grandma.

Mum gave a resigned sigh. 'Yes, yes I will – but I'm not sure . . .'

'Well, why don't we get the girls in here and see what they say,' said Mrs Duggery.

'Okay,' agreed Mum. She got up and went to the door, opened it and called her daughters. Within thirty seconds she came back to her seat.

'What's that you're holding?' she asked, sitting down again and seeing something on Mrs Duggery's lap.

'Thas the magic box.'

'Where did it come from?'

'I brought it with me.'

'But you weren't carrying anything when you came in!' exclaimed Mum, her face incredulous. She looked across at Grandma – who looked equally surprised.

'It just appeared on her lap!' said Grandma.

Mum's mouth dropped open.

Mrs Duggery smiled enigmatically.

The Sprite Sisters came into the library – and gasped.

'Oh my goodness – there's the box!' cried Ariel, sitting down beside the tiny old lady.

'But – but – where *was* it?' asked Marina, flopping down the other side.

Flame frowned. 'Has it been in the house all the time?'

Mrs Duggery shook her head. 'No, I's brought it with me. Kept it safe.'

Mum looked absolutely baffled. If she had any doubts about Mrs Duggery's magic, they had been dispelled. She sat, staring at the old lady.

Marina grinned at her mother. 'See, Mum, we told you she was magic!'

Mum put her head in her hands and stared down at the carpet. 'It's all very, very strange indeed . . .' she said, in a quiet voice.

Mrs Duggery handed Flame the box. Mum looked up, noticed the look of relief on her daughter's face – and felt glad for her.

Flame sat down on the carpet beside the fire and put the box on the low table between the sofas. Everyone leaned forward, as Flame prised open the lid.

Her face lit up. 'It's here! The plan is here!'

'Thank heavens for that!' said Marina.

Gently, Flame took out the secret plan and unfolded it on the table. 'Look – the mark has changed again! It's got four lines now – it's become a Crossed Circle with eight sections!'

Mrs Duggery nodded at Flame, her eyes glittering.

'Is this what you were expecting to happen?' asked Flame.

Mrs Duggery nodded again and took the last chocolate biscuit.

'Fab fantastic!' said Ariel, peering at the plan, then smiling at her mother. 'It's so exciting!'

'Yes,' said Mum, hesitantly.

'Let's see!' said Ash, moving closer.

The four Sprite Sisters pored over the secret plan, their faces alive.

Mum laughed – happy to see her daughters look so happy. She looked across at Grandma, who smiled back.

'So, Mrs Duggery – what does it mean?' asked Flame. 'What is it we have to find or do?'

'The treasure of Sprite Towers int a box a gold. No, it's summat you can do to put balance back in ter the family. Now, Glenda, she's tipped it all out a' balance. Thas all gorn dark and bad. But I reckon she want ter heal now.' She looked across at Grandma. 'What do you reckon, Marilyn? You saw her yesterday.'

Grandma considered this. 'Glenda *was* different,' she said. 'She let me into the house, for a start. Then she listened to what I had to say – and, most surprising of all, she didn't threaten me. That would never have happened before – but then I would never have gone to see her before. Also – surprisingly – she did not deny she had my money. She knew I was serious about getting it back, one way or the other.' Grandma looked thoughtful. 'The other thing is, I sensed she felt a little lost. There was a feeling of loneliness around her that I have never seen before. Perhaps it's just age, but she was different to how she used to be.'

Mrs Duggery nodded. 'Well, that sound ter me like thas time.'

'Time?' asked Grandma.

Mrs Duggery nodded again, then looked at Mum. 'Ottalie, I know you have yer doubts about the magic power, but how would you feel about askin' Glenda ter Sprite Towers ter do some magic with us?'

Mum's reaction was instant. 'I'm not having that evil woman in my house after all the damage she has done!' she cried.

Everyone looked at Mum. Her face was white with anger.

Mrs Duggery was silent. Then she said, 'I understand my dear, but what about if I tol' yer thas the only way we could do this magic?'

'*I don't want anyone to do any more magic!*' exclaimed Mum.

Mrs Duggery's eyes glinted. The room felt tense in the silence that followed. The Sprite Sisters looked from Mrs Duggery to their mother and back.

Mum gulped. 'Well, I'll think about it and talk with Colin.'

Mrs Duggery sat back on the sofa. 'Well, we got a few days,' she said.

For a while nobody spoke. Then Ash looked over at Mrs

Duggery and asked, 'Are you going to stay with us?'

'Please do!' said Ariel, looking up at the old lady. She looked across at her mother. 'Can Mrs Duggery stay for Christmas, Mum?'

Everyone looked at Mum. She turned toward the fire and sighed.

I've just been ambushed, she thought. Mrs Duggery is not going to go away and the girls are not going to stop pressing me. I can see I am not going to be able to stop this magic stuff. At least the girls look happy again . . .

She turned and smiled – a little wanly – at Mrs Duggery. 'Of course, Mrs Duggery,' she said. 'You must spend Christmas with us. You are most welcome.'

Mrs Duggery smiled at Mum. 'Thank you, my dear. Thas very kind a' you and would be right nice.'

'Goodie!' said Ash, smiling.

Ariel giggled. 'We'll need to get lots of chocolate biscuits, Mum!'

Mum laughed. 'I expect we can manage that.'

When Dad walked in from work that evening he was greeted by a smiling family. It was as if a new mood had swept through the house. The gloom had lifted from Sprite Towers and the anger dispelled.

'Welcome,' he said to Mrs Duggery, with a warm smile.

'Thank yer, Colin,' she said, with a twinkly smile.

Whilst Mum and Grandma cooked supper, he and Mrs Duggery sat by the fire and talked. She told him about some of the history of the family and how she had lived at Sprite

Towers when she was a child.

Then she told him about the magic she wanted them all to do.

'I'll talk to Ottalie about it,' he agreed.

That night, when everyone had gone up to bed, Mum and Dad sat together on the sofa by the fire.

Dad listened as Mum explained what had happened earlier and Mrs Duggery's request to do some more magic. Grandma had already explained to him about Glenda's apparent change of heart.

'There's a lot to think about,' said Dad, gazing at the fire.

They were silent for a while, then he said, 'If Mrs Duggery and the girls can do some sort of magic that will restore the balance in the family, that seems to me a good thing. It's a positive step for all the family relationships.'

'She said the girls would be a lot safer after that,' added Mum.

'Even better,' said Dad.

Mum pushed her blond wavy hair back from her face. 'It's all so strange to me. In some ways, I feel I'm no longer in charge of the house. It's as if Sprite Towers isn't ours.'

Dad smiled. 'Perhaps Sidney Sprite wanted it for all of us. But you shouldn't worry. You run this house so well, Ottalie – like clockwork. Everybody knows that. And you're a wonderful mother. It's just that Mrs Duggery knows about the magic – the other side of things that you and I are not part of in our girls' lives. But it doesn't mean they love us less.'

'You're right,' said Mum, with a sigh. 'The other thing is I feel uneasy when Mrs Duggery looks at me. It's as if she's looking straight through me. She seems to know what I'm thinking and everything about this place.'

Dad smiled. 'Yes, she's a bit scary. But she's very kind and she loves this family. She was telling me earlier about how she grew up here. Her father, George, was killed in France in the Great War – around the same time as Sidney's son, George, so she told me. She said that Sidney asked her mother, Elisa Duggery – his sister, who had been widowed in the Great War – to come and live with them, along with her daughter, Violet – Mrs Duggery. Young Violet and Elisa lived very happily at Sprite Towers. This place is in her bones. She is the last surviving Sprite relative we have – the only link back to that time.'

'It's amazing,' agreed Mum.

'She's well over a hundred!' laughed Dad.

'And still cycling that big old boneshaker bicycle!'

'She was telling me how she looked after both my father and me as children,' added Dad.

Mum giggled. 'I bet you were a lovely baby!'

'I was!'

'I wonder where she goes when she cycles off? Does she have anyone to look after her?'

Dad shook his head. 'I have no idea. She does not have any children, as far as I know.'

Mum smiled. 'Ariel said to me this afternoon that Sidney has told her he wants us to ask Mrs Duggery to come and live here at Sprite Towers. He says she's getting very old and she needs us to take care of her.'

'That would be the kind thing to do,' said Dad. 'But how would you feel about it?'

'It would be the kind thing to do, I agree,' said Mum. She looked sad. 'Having Mrs Duggery here reminds me that I don't have magic power – and I will never be able to share that with my daughters.'

'But you've got so many things you do share!' exclaimed Dad. 'Look at all the music! That's a huge part of their lives and it's all down to your support and inspiration. Think of that.'

Mum smiled. 'Yes, that's true.'

'We each give and do what we can,' said Dad.

'Hm,' said Mum, snuggling up to him.

Dad drew her close. 'I'd let Mrs Duggery and the girls do what they have to do.'

'I feel very uncomfortable about having Glenda in the house, though,' said Mum.

Dad frowned and scratched his chin. 'It would make it much easier if she returns the money first.'

'I don't suppose she'd dare show her face otherwise,' said Mum. 'And I think I'd be very tempted to clonk her with a rolling pin, after all the hurt she has caused!'

Dad laughed. 'Well, Mrs Duggery seems to have it all worked out. And I'm glad that Verena and the girls are getting on so well.'

They were quiet for a while, gazing at the fire.

Then Mum said, 'Ariel also said that Sidney had told her that when they've done this magic, that Mrs Duggery will get a lot older very suddenly, as it will take so much of her magic.'

'Oh dear,' said Dad, with a sad face.

'So we must look after her,' said Mum.

'Yes – yes, of course,' agreed Dad. 'We would have done anyway.'

Mum smiled.

'You know what?' said Dad.

'What?'

'I think we should sit back and let things take their course with the magic. Let Glenda and Verena come. Mrs Duggery will make sure no harm comes to anyone.'

'You really think that?'

'Yes, I do,' said Dad.

'Okay,' said Mum. 'It goes against everything I have ever believed, but I can see it matters an awful lot to you all. The girls looked so happy when the box appeared.'

'We'll have a much more peaceful Christmas, that's for sure,' said Dad, with a smile.

CHAPTER SIXTEEN

CONVINCING GLENDA

'DON'T BE *ridiculous!*' spat Glenda, when Verena told her that Mrs Duggery wanted her to do some magic at Sprite Towers. '*I'm not going to do anything with the Sprites!*'

It was Thursday morning and Verena had been talking to Flame and Marina on the phone.

'But, Grandma . . .' Verena's voice trailed off, as Glenda spun round to look at her.

'I've done some dreadful things to that family!' cried Glenda. 'How on earth can they want me to share their magic?'

'Mrs Duggery said it would be a special magic that would heal the whole family – everybody.'

Glenda's eyes narrowed further. 'Well, I don't care what it

is you want me to do, or how important you think it is. *The answer is no!'*

'But we need you!'

'Need me?'

'Yes!' cried Verena. 'Mrs Duggery says we need you to create the balance in the family.'

'Well, maybe I don't want to be the balance in the family!' shouted Glenda.

To this, Verena had no answer. They turned away from each other. Glenda was shaking with anger.

Verena put her hands on her hips and looked at her grandmother, with a sense of resolve. 'I'd like to go over to Sprite Towers this morning – and they've said I could. It's snowing again, so please would you take me.'

Glenda grabbed her car keys off the kitchen counter. 'Let's go, then,' she said, moving quickly towards the door. She was only too pleased to get rid of her granddaughter that morning. The last thing she wanted was a lecture on the Sprite family, when she had the issue of Marilyn Sprite's money on her mind.

Ten minutes later, they drew up the long driveway. Verena hopped out of the car, a big smile suddenly on her face. As she raced towards the front door, Glenda pulled away.

Verena was happy to be back at Sprite Towers. Within a minute she was standing by the Aga, laughing with the Sprites. Mrs Duggery sat, watching her.

She had met the magical old lady before. A few months before, Mrs Duggery had found Verena and Marina going up to one of the towers one afternoon – and she'd been very cross with them. It was at the time when Glenda was asking Verena to spy on the Sprite family – and Mrs Duggery knew exactly what she was up to.

Today she found Mrs Duggery more friendly, but no less terrifying. 'It's her eyes,' she whispered to Marina. 'She seems to look right through me. It's as if she knows what I am thinking.'

'She does,' agreed Marina, in a matter-of-fact voice.

A few minutes later, the Sprite Sisters and Verena carried mugs of thick hot chocolate up to Flame's room and sat down on the carpet.

Flame drew out the magic box and unfolded the plan on the floor between them. 'You see that mark there,' she said to Verena. 'That's appeared, bit by bit, in the last few days. It's the sign of the Crossed Circle.'

'Wow!' said Verena, leaning over to look at it. 'What does it mean?'

'Mrs Duggery says it's something to do with the treasure we have to find,' replied Flame.

Verena sat up and looked at Flame. 'So where are we all going to do this magic?'

The Sprite Sisters looked at one another. 'We haven't talked about that,' said Flame.

'Has Mrs Duggery said anything?' asked Verena.

'No,' said the Sprite Sisters, looking from one to the other again.

'We often stand in the tower when we do magic,' said Marina. 'Why don't you ask your stone, Ash?'

Ash pulled the magic stone out of her jeans pocket and held it on her palm. When she said the words 'East Tower', the stone did not react. But when she said the words, 'West Tower', the stone emitted a soft blue pulsing light. 'Look – it likes that!' she said.

'So we know where to start,' said Verena.

'But Mrs Duggery's not here to help us,' said Ariel. 'She's busy helping Mummy.'

'We could still go up and have a look,' said Flame, folding up the plan. 'Come on.'

A moment later, they were all running up the staircase.

'West Tower,' said Flame, turning right along the attics corridor. At the end, she grabbed the handle on the rickety wooden door and yanked it open.

'It's the first time I've ever been up here!' said Verena, climbing the rickety stairs.

'Mrs Duggery stopped us last time, remember,' laughed Marina, behind her.

And there they were, standing in the round tower room. Under their feet was the oak floor and above them was the huge, glass-domed roof.

Verena looked around the room and up at the glass dome. 'It's amazing!' she exclaimed.

'It's *freezing*!' shuddered Marina, despite her thick woolly jumper. 'Urgh!' She rubbed her arms and wiggled about to keep warm.

'You can see our breath in the air, it's so cold up here!' laughed Ash, waving her hands in the mist in front of her face.

In the centre of the room, Flame stood looking at the plan.

The others began to look around the walls.

A moment later, Ash pointed up. 'There's a Crossed Circle carved into the bricks up here! Look there, about five metres up.'

Flame looked up at the Crossed Circle, which was about the span of her hand in size. 'You're right,' she said. 'That's the north wall, there.'

'And one up here at the south side,' said Marina, standing opposite Ash.

'And here,' said Ariel, standing at the west with her head tilted back.

Verena walked to the east-facing wall. 'And up here, too,' she said, pointing her finger.

'They're all about the same height,' said Marina, looking round.

'So that's the four directions,' said Flame, looking again at the plan.

'I wonder why we've never noticed the marks before?' asked Ariel.

'Maybe they weren't here before,' said Marina.

Flame moved her hand up and down, north to south and back and forth, east to west. 'So the two main lines would cut across this way and that way,' she said. 'Which means that the two secondary lines run north-west to south-east and north-east to south-west.'

Within a minute, the five girls had established where the lines of the Crossed Circle would run.

'Now what?' asked Verena, shivering in her pink cashmere jumper.

Marina waved her hand towards the middle of the floor. 'Ash, why don't you put your magic stone down there and see what happens.'

Ash pulled out her stone and laid it on the centre of the round floor. Then everyone moved towards the wall and stood, waiting.

'Let's stand by the wall in each of our four directions,' said Marina.

'Good idea,' said Flame. Marina stood still, while Flame moved to the east, Ash to the west and Ariel to the north.

'Where shall I stand?' asked Verena.

'Here, between me and Ariel – in the north-east,' said Flame.

'How do you know?'

'The north-east is the place of Action,' explained Flame. 'And if your magic power is about conducting things, it's about movement. And Action is about movement.'

Verena smiled and stood against the wall halfway between Flame and Ariel. 'Good thinking,' she said.

They all stood still, looked at the magic stone in the centre of the room – and waited. For several minutes nothing happened. The smooth, round grey-brown stone sat on the floor. The Sprite Sisters looked at one another and shrugged. Verena looked from one sister to another. The only sound was everyone's teeth chattering with cold.

'Nothing's happening,' said Verena.

'Yes it is,' said Ash, as a faint blue light began to pulse from the stone.

The girls watched, fascinated, as the light got stronger and stronger, second by second. Blue light whooshed out over the floor, across the wooden boards.

'My hands are beginning to tingle,' said Ash, wiggling her fingers.

'So are mine,' said Ariel, her eyes wide.

They waited and waited, all the time watching the stone.

After what felt like an age, Ariel shouted, 'Look at the floor!'

'There are lines appearing!' shouted Ash.

'Don't move!' shouted Flame.

As she said this, the sign of the Crossed Circle formed on the floor in radiating lines of bright blue light. The circle of light spanned the room, reaching to within about half a metre of the wall.

The girls laughed in amazement – and stood absolutely still.

'It's the eight sections of the Crossed Circle!' said Flame. 'Just like the plan here!'

'What are we supposed to do?' asked Verena, shuddering with cold.

'I think we're meant to stand in each of the sections and summon our magic,' said Flame.

'But there are only five of us here,' said Marina.

'Maybe not now,' said Flame. 'Maybe it's just showing us.'

Ariel frowned. 'Mrs Duggery and Glenda would make seven.'

'*If* I can persuade my grandmother!' said Verena, with a sharp laugh. 'She's adamant she won't join in.'

'But even with Glenda – who's the eighth person?' asked Ash.

The girls looked from one to another.

'Charles?' suggested Marina.

'Could be,' agreed Flame. 'He has got magic powers.'

'What about Grandma?' said Ariel. 'I think it's her.'

'*Grandma?*' said Marina, screwing up her face.

'She used to have magical powers,' said Ariel.

'Maybe they'd come back for this magic,' suggested Ash.

'That would be eight Sprite females with magical powers,' said Flame, with a thoughtful look. As she said this, the bright blue light began to fade.

Within half a minute, all trace of the Crossed Circle had disappeared.

'That was amazing!' said Verena, moving towards the centre of the room, bending down and touching the floorboards. 'It's completely vanished!'

Ash picked up her stone from the centre of the floor and put it back in her pocket.

'Let's go down and tell Mrs Duggery,' said Flame.

'Let's go down before we all freeze to *death* . . .' grumbled Marina.

'Last one down's a sissy!' shouted Ariel, turning towards the door.

With that, the five girls raced down the rickety steps, round and round the wide mahogany staircase, through the hallway and burst through the kitchen door in a big heap.

A minute later, the Sprite Sisters and Verena stood huddled around the Aga, trying to warm up. They didn't tell Mum what they had been doing, as she warmed some milk and made more mugs of hot chocolate. Grandma put out a plate of chocolate biscuits.

Then the girls, Mum, Grandma and Mrs Duggery sat around the big oak table. The girls grabbed chocolate biscuits, but Mrs Duggery was faster.

'That's the whole packet!' said Mum, staring at the empty plate.

Later that day, Verena sat and talked to Mrs Duggery beside the fire. The tiny old lady in the lilac knitted hat watched Glenda Glass's granddaughter with her glinting eyes.

Verena watched Mrs Duggery, part curious, part in awe – and told her what had been happening at The Oaks.

Mrs Duggery listened and nodded. When Verena finished speaking, she said, 'You tell yer grandmother tha' she *has* ter come. Thas the way she can settle things. Tell her she either goes ter prison – or she comes here an' does this magic ter heal the whole family. You tell her that. She must give back the money an' she must come here ter help us. Then things'ull mend once agin.'

Verena watched the tiny old lady and listened hard.

A few seconds later Mrs Duggery said, 'Thas called "atonement". When yer done summat wrong – an' Glenda has done a lot of bad things – then yer have to make up fer it. An' this is what yer grandmother has ter do now. You tell her that from me. Tell her if she wan' some peace in her life, she has ter come ter Sprite Towers an' do the magic.'

Verena nodded, thoughtfully. 'I will, Mrs Duggery,' she said. 'I will tell her this evening.'

* * *

Later, at The Oaks, Glenda sat by the fire with a glass of cold white wine. Verena sat opposite with her raspberry smoothie. They both stared at the flames, preoccupied.

Then, with a quiet intensity, Verena began to talk. Despite her grandmother's protestations, she insisted that she speak. 'Please listen for my sake, Grandma, if not for your own,' she said. 'Please do this for me.'

Glenda Glass sighed a long, deep sigh. 'All right,' she said and leaned back on the sofa.

Little by little, Verena told her grandmother of the magic she had seen at Sprite Towers and what Mrs Duggery had told her.

Glenda sipped her wine with a thoughtful look, from time to time looking across at Verena. Mostly, though, she stared at the fire.

As Verena got to the part about atonement, her grandmother looked at her with eyes that sent a shiver down her back. But still she carried on.

Every time she thought Glenda would get up and walk off, she said, 'Please listen for my sake, Grandma.'

It was when Verena said, 'Mrs Duggery says you have to learn to dream again', that Glenda Glass found herself really listening.

Is that what I have forgotten, she wondered. I have forgotten to dream . . .

As she looked across at her granddaughter's clear blue eyes and her young, bright face, Glenda found herself aware of the feelings of another human being.

Verena has a dream, she thought – a dream that the family

can be whole once again. And now she has asked me to dream. What do I dream of? I don't dream . . .

Glenda gazed at the flames, then said, 'When I was a little girl I remember Sidney Sprite used to say, "Dream your dreams awake".'

Verena smiled. 'That's a lovely idea – I like that. Dream your dreams awake . . .'

Glenda stared at the fire. Flames cleanse, she thought. Could I have a new start in my life? Would that really be possible, after all the terrible things I have done?

After a while, Verena said, 'So you will come?'

Glenda looked round at her and said, 'I don't know. There is a lot to think about. And there's a lot of pride involved.'

Verena was intelligent enough to know when to leave things be. There would be no gain in pressing her grandmother any further.

But now she had her grandmother's attention, she was curious. 'Tell me about your life, Grandma,' she said. 'I know nothing about you – and I'd really like to.'

As Glenda Glass looked across at her granddaughter, her face clouded with sorrow. Verena waited.

Then Glenda began to talk. She talked of the bitterness her mother and grandmother had felt towards Sidney Sprite, of how they had struggled in their lives – and how they had used the dark magic power to help them get what they wanted.

She told Verena about her jealousy of Marilyn Sprite when they were young dancers and how they had battled on the dark London street. She told her of her four marriages and four dead husbands. Then she talked about her son.

'Even when Stephen was born I felt empty,' she said. 'It's only been these last few months that I have come to know and love him. Imagine that. All those years . . . all those wasted years.'

Verena sat, sad and shocked, by the fire. 'Have you talked to Daddy about it?'

Glenda shook her head very slowly. 'No . . .' she said in a voice that was almost a whisper.

Verena sat forward and looked her grandmother in the eye. 'But now you have a chance to make up for all of that.'

Glenda laughed a short, hollow laugh. 'You really believe that?'

Verena nodded.

'You are so young, Verena. You know nothing of the world and how hard things are out there – how cruel life can be.'

Verena sat up straight. 'I know what it is to feel lonely. I know what it is to feel sad and alone. And I also know what it is to feel loved – and to have family and friends who care about me.' She looked towards the fire and said in a quiet voice, 'I know which feeling I prefer.'

Glenda Glass met her granddaughter's eyes. And, for the first time since she'd arrived at The Oaks in June, there was warmth in her smile.

Then she looked away – a worried look passing over her face. Verena waited.

'I've never been frightened – but I'm frightened now,' said Glenda. 'What will your father do when he finds out the truth?'

Verena met her gaze again. 'I don't know, Grandma.'

They were silent for a while. Then Verena said, 'Perhaps we could wait to tell Daddy. He doesn't need to know yet.'

Glenda frowned. 'If everyone knows, then he would have to know.'

'Yes, maybe – but not immediately. Not with Mummy coming home. Why don't we just do one thing at a time – and see what happens.'

Glenda sighed a long sigh.

They were silent again for some while.

Then Glenda got up off the sofa. 'Time for bed now,' she said.

Verena came towards her grandmother and kissed her on the cheek. ''Night,' she said and went up to bed.

'Good night, dear,' said Glenda, touching her cheek where Verena had kissed her.

For the next few minutes, Glenda made safe the fire, turned off the lights and shut the doors. Then she walked up the stairs to her bedroom.

There she sat down at her desk and turned on her laptop. As it whirred into action, she watched the reflection of her face on the dark screen.

CHAPTER SEVENTEEN

GLENDA RETREATS

GRANDMA COULDN'T believe her ears on Friday afternoon, when the bank telephoned to say that all the money that had been taken out of her account four years ago had been put back in. In addition, a considerable amount of interest had also been paid, amounting to what she would have earned had the money been in her account during that time.

'It's all back!' said Grandma, with a look of enormous relief.

'Thank heavens!' said Dad, putting his arm around her shoulder.

'It's wonderful news, Marilyn!' said Mum, giving her a big hug.

'Fantastic!' said the Sprite Sisters.

'And just three days till Christmas Eve,' said Dad.

Grandma looked stunned. 'The bank said the money was transferred from an offshore account, all in one go, apparently – including the interest.'

'So, do we assume it was Glenda who sent it?' asked Mum.

Grandma nodded thoughtfully. 'I think so, dear. I can't see who else would have put such a huge sum into my account. And just a few days after I'd spoken to her, too.'

'Has she been in touch?' asked Dad.

'No,' replied Grandma. 'I've heard nothing from her at all.'

'Verena says that Glenda is locked in her bedroom and hasn't come down yet,' said Marina.

'She's worried,' added Flame. 'She says Glenda is never ill.'

'Is Verena all right?' asked Mum.

'She says her grandmother won't answer her or open the door,' said Flame.

'Maybe Glenda is really ill,' said Mum.

'She might be dead!' said Ariel, wide-eyed.

Flame shrugged. 'Or just feeling sorry for herself.'

Dad laughed. 'Racked with remorse, you mean?'

'Yes – huddled under the duvet, whimpering,' smiled Flame. 'Isn't that what a cheat should do?'

'Nobody respects a cheat,' agreed Dad.

'Nor a wimp,' said Flame, dismissively.

Dad laughed. 'Still, at least Glenda has *given back* the money,' he said. Then he turned to look at Mrs Duggery, sitting at the kitchen table. 'What do you think, Violet?'

She looked back at him with her dark, glinty eyes.

'In life, tha's your own face you have to look at in the mirror,' she said. 'Inside, we all know whether we done right or wrong. Thas a start for Glenda – I will say that. An' I'm right glad fer Marilyn – and all a' you. Thas' a big relief for the family.'

Dad smiled. 'Yes, it is,' he agreed.

'But what about the magic?' asked Ariel, quietly, sitting down beside Mrs Duggery.

'When will we be able to find the treasure of Sprite Towers?' asked Ash.

Mrs Duggery stared at the chocolate biscuit she was about to eat. 'All we can do is wait,' she said – and ate the biscuit.

'But you said we had to do it before Christmas,' said Ariel, frowning.

'I did that,' agreed Mrs Duggery.

'Well?'

'Thas a deep hole,' said Mrs Duggery.

'What is?'

'A well,' said Mrs Duggery, with a glinty smile.

Ariel laughed. 'You know what I meant!'

Mrs Duggery smiled as she took another chocolate biscuit.

Ariel rested her chin on her hands and sighed. 'Oh dear, I don't think we're going to ever find the treasure . . .'

She looked round at Mrs Duggery, hoping this would elicit a response, but the old lady was absorbed in her biscuit.

By late afternoon, Verena Glass was getting really worried. Her grandmother had still not appeared – she had been locked in her room since the evening before. Nor would she even answer, when Verena knocked on the door.

Verena turned on some lights, but the house felt dark and empty – and she felt very alone. Should I call the police or the doctor, she wondered.

Instead, she called Flame – again. 'She's still up there,' she said.

'I'm sure she's all right. She's just, you know – a bit down.'

'Hm,' said Verena, looking out into the dark.

'Have you got some food and stuff?' asked Flame.

'Yes, yes – the fridge is well stocked,' replied Verena. 'It's just really weird being here alone, like this.'

'Do you want to come over here?'

'I think I'd better stay here in case Grandma is ill and does need me,' said Verena.

'Well, you must call us if you need anything,' said Flame. 'Mum and Dad can be there in a matter of minutes.'

'Thank you,' said Verena.

'Have you told your parents?'

'They just called,' replied Verena. 'I told them Grandma may have a virus. Mum suggested I call the doctor, but I told her Grandma didn't want the doctor. And I told her that your parents were in touch. So Mum said okay and that they'll be home very soon.'

'Yes, it's only three days away now,' said Flame. She was silent for a second, then said, 'We haven't got long to do the magic, if we're to do it before Christmas as Mrs Duggery said we should.'

'I'd forgotten about that,' said Verena.

'Well, you've got a lot on your mind,' said Flame.

That evening, Mum rang Verena at The Oaks and asked if everything was all right.

'In returning Marilyn's money, your grandmother has done something immense,' said Mum. 'She's had to admit something profound to herself, and it may take a little time to face the world again. She's in shock – you know, when people have a big fright. It can leave you feeling very tired. I'm sure she'll come downstairs tomorrow. Let her rest tonight and don't worry. But if you need us, remember we are just down the road.'

'But she may be dead up there,' said Verena, in a tremulous voice.

'Mrs Duggery thinks that your grandmother is okay, but that she needs to rest,' said Mum. 'And Mrs Duggery seems to be right about an awful lot of things.'

Verena laughed softly.

'Not long to go now,' said Mum. 'Chin up.'

'Thank you, Ottalie,' said Verena. 'Good night.'

On Saturday morning, Glenda unlocked her door. Verena came into the bedroom and drew back the curtains. Pale winter light streamed into the room. Glenda lay in her bed, silent and staring into space.

A little later, Verena called Ottalie Sprite and asked her what to do.

'Your grandmother needs to keep warm, drink lots and eat something,' said Ottalie. 'First of all, make her a cup of tea and a hot water bottle. Then I should take her a small bowl of porridge with some honey on the top. She needs to drink, too, so I should put a glass and a jug of water beside her bed.'

With a huge sense of relief, Verena raced up and down with trays of food and drink and the bottle. She made her grandmother sit up before she handed her the cup of tea. Glenda took it and sipped it, but did not seem to want to speak. Her face was grey and her eyes unfocused.

Then Verena gave Glenda the porridge and sat down on the end of the bed.

She suddenly felt very aware of how old and unwell her grandmother looked. She had never seen Glenda look less than elegant at all times. Now she looked like an old lady, her hair dishevelled and her thin hands gripping the spoon.

When she finished, Verena took the tray away. Then Glenda lay back against the pillows and closed her eyes.

So the day passed. Glenda lay silently staring into space or asleep.

When Stephen and Zoe rang to ask how things were, Verena was able to say that Glenda had eaten a little food and was resting.

'Well done, darling,' said her mother. 'I'm so proud of you.'

Verena wiped away the tear that ran down her face.

'Soon be home now,' said Zoe.

'I can't wait,' said Verena, wiping away another tear.

'Nor can I,' said Zoe – seven thousand miles away and wiping away even bigger tears.

A little while later, Verena ran her grandmother a hot bath and put out warm towels. Glenda pulled on her dressing gown and walked slowly through to her bathroom. Her face was ashen white and her body stiff.

By the time Glenda had finished and returned to bed, Verena had prepared a hot meal. Glenda sat up as Verena placed the tray in front of her.

'It was a chicken dish I found in the fridge,' explained Verena. 'I read the instructions and put it in the oven. And I rang Ottalie to find out what to do with the vegetables.'

Glenda turned to her granddaughter with the saddest eyes. Verena's heart churned.

'Eat, Grandma,' said Verena. 'Please eat.'

Glenda picked up the fork and began to eat, very slowly. Verena watched her, silent.

Finally, when Glenda had finished eating, Verena took away the tray.

'Thank you for looking after me so well,' whispered Glenda.

Verena gulped. 'I've been worried about you.'

Glenda reached out her hand on the top of the bed. Verena put the tray on the floor, sat down on the bed and took her grandmother's hand.

Glenda turned her face away, and whispered in a voice only just audible, 'Tell them I'm sorry – the Sprites.'

'I will,' said Verena, squeezing her grandmother's hand.

They stayed like that for several minutes.

Then Verena said, 'You must rest again now, Grandma.'

Glenda nodded and turned over on her right side. Verena pulled the duvet over her grandmother's shoulders, put out the light, picked up the tray and went downstairs.

In the kitchen, she sat on a stool and wept.

When Ottalie called again, Verena said, 'Grandma's eaten some food and I'm all right.'

'Well done – you're doing really well,' said Ottalie.

'Ottalie . . .'

'Yes?'

'Grandma says . . . Grandma said to say sorry to you all.'

Ottalie Sprite was silent. Verena waited.

Eventually Ottalie said, 'Tell her that her apology is accepted.'

'I will – and thank you for everything you've done.'

'You are very welcome, dear. Now get some rest and don't worry. I'll call you in the morning.'

'Good night,' said Verena, sniffing.

Then she turned off the Christmas tree lights, bolted the front door and walked up the elegant staircase. The house seemed huge and empty.

We need people in this house, she thought. We need laughter – and a dog. I will ask Mummy and Daddy if we can have a puppy like Archie.

As she climbed into bed, she remembered the robin that her grandmother had killed with her magic, only a few days before. She remembered the look of anger in her grandmother's eyes, her sarcastic voice and the finger pointing at the little bird.

Then she thought of how her grandmother looked now.

She's changed, she thought. And I'm glad.

And with that, she turned out the light and fell into a deep sleep.

That night, as Glenda Glass lay in her bed, she dreamed. She dreamed of shaking hands with Marilyn Sprite, of the Sprite family smiling at her as they stood around the Christmas tree. She dreamed of Mrs Duggery with her white hair swept into a bun at the back of her neck. She dreamed of Stephen standing with his arm around her shoulders – and saw herself looking up to him and feeling a huge smile inside. She dreamed of feeling a sense of inner warmth that she had never felt before.

When she woke early the next morning, the pillows were wet with tears.

As she pulled herself up the bed, she thought, I dreamed. I'm sure I dreamed . . .

She sat, staring into the darkness and pushed back pale blond hair from her face. Then she lay back down on the damp pillows and fell into a gentle sleep.

All through Sunday, Glenda stayed in bed, most of the time asleep. Verena ran up and down with trays of food and drink and fresh hot water bottles. In the afternoon – worn out – she laid down on top of the bed beside her grandmother and fell asleep.

Glenda got out of bed and put a blanket over the sleeping girl. Then she climbed back in and watched over her granddaughter, tears pouring down her face. From time to time, she stroked Verena's long blond hair and thought how beautiful she was.

When Verena awoke, the moon was rising in the inky black sky.

'I must have fallen asleep,' she said, sitting up and shivering.

'Ooh, it's cold.' She looked at her grandmother. 'How long have I been here?'

'A few hours,' said Glenda, in a gentle voice. 'You must have been very tired. You went out like a light.'

Verena laughed. 'I did! I've never done so much running up and down stairs!'

Glenda smiled. 'Thank you, my dear. I appreciate your kindness.'

Verena reached up and gave her grandmother a kiss on the cheek. 'You're very welcome, Grandma.'

They were silent for a few seconds, then Verena got off the bed and said, 'You've been up here since Friday evening, Grandma – and it's now Sunday evening. How about coming down for supper?'

Glenda smiled. 'I'd like that.'

'I'll go down and light the fire,' said Verena. As she was about to leave the room, she turned. 'I relayed your message to Ottalie Sprite, Grandma.'

Glenda looked down at her hands.

'She said, "Apology accepted".'

Glenda nodded thoughtfully, but said nothing. Just as Verena was about to leave, Glenda said, 'Please don't say anything to your parents.'

Verena waited. Then she said, 'I won't, Grandma. That's up to you, when you're ready.'

Glenda covered her mouth with her hand and closed her eyes.

'I'll see you downstairs in a minute, then,' said Verena.

As she went downstairs, she checked her phone. Umpteen

messages had arrived from Flame and Marina. *How is Glenda?* they asked. *And is she ready to do the magic?*

We've only got tomorrow! texted Flame. *Mrs Duggery said we had to do it before Christmas!*

Oh Gawd, thought Verena. I'd forgotten all about the magic. Shall I mention it to Grandma? Will it make her angry and spoil things?

For a few minutes, she dithered about in the kitchen, not sure what she was doing.

Then Glenda walked in, in her dressing gown. 'What's happened?' she said, seeing Verena's distraught face.

Verena looked at the floor. 'It's the Sprite Sisters,' she said, hurriedly. 'They've reminded me about the magic. Mrs Duggery said we had to do it before Christmas. Mummy and Daddy will be back tomorrow – and I don't know what to do!'

She turned to look at Glenda, half expecting her grandmother to blast her with anger.

But Glenda stood still, her hands in her dressing gown pockets. Then she said in a quiet voice, 'I will come with you in the morning, if that's convenient for the Sprites – and we will do the magic.'

Verena's mouth fell open. 'Will you?' she said. For a few seconds, she stood completely still.

Glenda nodded. 'Yes.'

'Oh, that would be amazing!' Verena burst out – and rushed to hug her grandmother.

'Careful!' said Glenda, smiling, but almost bowled off her feet.

Verena laughed. 'They'll all be so pleased! I'll tell them now!'

She called Flame's number. '*Flame!*' she said. '*Flame! Grandma has agreed to do the magic!* We'll be there in the morning. Is that all right with you?'

She waited as Flame ran down to ask her parents. 'She's just asking,' she said to Glenda. Then, 'Okay! Great! We'll see you at ten o'clock!' And she clicked off the phone.

She turned to Glenda. 'Flame says that her mother has agreed they can do the magic. It seems Mrs Duggery has persuaded her.'

She came towards her grandmother and wrapped her arms around her neck.

'Thank you so much!' she said. 'I am *so* excited about using my magic power!'

'Just as long as you never hurt a robin,' said Glenda, with a sad smile.

Verena stood back and shook her head. 'I'd never do that, Grandma.'

'No, I'm sure you never would.'

'Nor will you ever again.'

Glenda put her hand over her mouth and gave a little sob. 'No, never again.' She whispered. 'Never again.'

CHAPTER EIGHTEEN

NEW MAGIC

MONDAY MORNING shone bright and clear. Another sharp frost had left the trees icy white and the ground hard.

The Sprite Sisters were up early, their faces shining with excitement.

'Christmas Eve!' shouted Ariel.

'Magic!' shouted Marina, as they ran over the wide rolling lawn to the stables.

They waved to Dad, who was towing another load of firewood to the house, behind his little ride-on tractor.

Archie ran round and round in circles on the grass, carrying a stick in his mouth. Bert lolloped along sniffing things.

The two girls opened the hutch doors, filled up the rabbits' and guinea pigs' feed dishes and water bottles and added fresh straw to their bedding. All the time, they were chattering with excitement.

In the house, Ariel was feeding her gerbils. Flame was helping her mother to mix the chestnut stuffing for the turkey in a huge bowl on the kitchen table. Grandma was peeling what looked like a whole bucket of potatoes and Mrs Duggery was peeling onions, carrots and parsnips.

'What a feast this will be!' smiled Flame.

Pudding, the tabby cat, looked up from his cushion on the Windsor chair beside the Aga, licked a paw and went back to sleep.

Just before ten o'clock, the Sprite Sisters got tidied up and waited in the kitchen – almost jumping up and down with excitement. Mrs Duggery and Grandma took off their aprons and washed their hands. Mum filled the kettle and put it on the Aga.

'I think we'd be better to get straight on and have coffee afterwards,' said Grandma.

'Okay,' said Mum, taking off the kettle. She looked across at her mother-in-law. 'How do you feel, Marilyn?'

Grandma sighed – gave a small smile. 'A little strange – just nerves, perhaps.'

'It must feel very odd after all these years – with all that has passed between you and Glenda.'

'Yes, it does,' agreed Grandma. 'And not having been able to use my magic power for so many years, since I lost it in the battle with Glenda.'

Flame came up beside her, took her arm and gave her

grandmother a kiss on her cheek. 'Ready?' she asked.

Grandma smiled and patted her hand. 'Ready,' she said, as the doorbell rang.

For a second, everybody stood stock-still. Then Mum walked through the hallway and opened the big front door. Grandma and the girls followed.

Outside, Verena and Glenda waited nervously.

'Good morning,' smiled Mum. 'Come in.'

Verena held Glenda under the arm as they walked into the hallway. The Sprite family stood, waiting.

There was a moment of stillness. Then Glenda walked towards Marilyn Sprite. 'Marilyn,' said Glenda, holding out her right hand. 'I have an apology to make.'

Grandma took Glenda's hand and gripped it. Their eyes met: Grandma's green and Glenda's blue.

'I'm so sorry,' said Glenda. '*For everything.*'

There was silence in the big hallway. Glenda looked round at Ottalie and the Sprite Sisters. 'I'm so sorry,' she said again. Then she looked back at Marilyn Sprite, still holding her hand.

'Thank you, Glenda,' said Marilyn. The two older women smiled at each other in the way that people smile when much has happened and they know that things will never be the same again.

A wave of poignant emotion – a mixture of happiness and sadness – swept over the group. Ariel, wide-eyed, took hold of her mother's hand. Mrs Duggery's eyes glinted. Flame looked across at Verena, noted her nervous face – and smiled, encouragingly. Marina and Ash looked at one another.

The silence in the hallway was broken by Dad, as he pushed open the front door and carried in a big basket of logs. Archie and Bert followed him.

'Morning!' he said, cheerily.

Everyone looked round with a gulp of relief. Verena bent down to stroke Archie.

Dad put down the basket on the floor and came forward to greet Glenda.

'I hope you're feeling better now,' he said, shaking her hand and smiling his kind smile.

'Yes, thank you, Colin – much better,' she said, with a hesitant smile.

Dad looked round at his daughters. 'I gather you're off to do some magic in the tower,' he said.

There was a moment of awkward silence. Nobody moved, except to glance at Mum. She looked very uncomfortable.

Then Dad stepped forward, put his arm around Mum's shoulder and smiled down at her. She looked up at him, reassured, then turned to the others and said, 'Well, you'd better get going – Zoe and Stephen will be back in a few hours.'

'Good luck!' said Dad.

'Yes, good luck,' said Mum.

Dad turned to pick up the log basket and push open the door. Mum watched as her four daughters, Marilyn, Glenda, Mrs Duggery and Verena walked up the wide mahogany staircase. She was still standing there a minute later, a strange, wistful look on her face, when Dad came back.

'Glenda looks as if she's had all the stuffing knocked out of her,' he said, putting his arm around Mum's shoulders.

'Just what I was thinking, but she's lost that cold, imperious look of hers,' said Mum.

'I think she's genuinely sorry.'

'It certainly seems so.'

'Now, Ottalie, don't stand here worrying about the girls and the magic,' said Dad. 'They'll be fine.'

Mum laughed. 'No – too much to do to stand here all day.' She was silent for a moment, then looked up at Dad. 'It feels strange to be out here, when my daughters and mother-in-law are up in the tower.'

Dad smiled. 'Yes, it must.' Then he went on, 'I take it the Glass family will be joining us for lunch tomorrow, as well as Christmas Eve supper?'

'I was hoping you'd say that,' said Mum. 'They won't have anything prepared, as Glenda has been ill. Zoe won't be able to cook, anyhow, with a broken collar bone. We've more than enough food. I'll mention it when they come down.'

'Good,' said Dad.

'How long do you think they'll be up there?'

'My darling – I have no idea!' laughed Dad. 'Let's hope they finish before Stephen and Zoe arrive.'

The eight Sprite females stood in the circular West Tower room. High above them was the huge glass dome.

Glenda and Verena, both shivering with cold, looked up and around with a sense of awe.

'It's huge,' murmured Verena.

'It's freezing,' shuddered Marina.

Mrs Duggery looked at Flame. 'Now, the first thing we

got ter do is warm this room up a bit,' she said. 'Flame, can yer do tha' please.'

Everyone moved to the side of the round wall, as Flame stood in the centre of the room and held out her long arms. Raising her hands slightly above the level of her head, she pointed her index fingers, closed her eyes and turned slowly in a circle.

As Flame Sprite summoned her magic power of Fire, a gentle blue light began to glow around her hands.

'The air is warming!' said Verena.

'That's better,' said Marina. 'Nice and toasty.'

When the air in the tower room was really warm, Mrs Duggery said, 'That'll do nicely, thank yer, Flame.'

Flame lowered her hands.

'Amazing!' said Verena.

Flame looked across at Glenda. For the first time she had known her, Glenda's pale blue eyes looked approving. She smiled hesitantly at Flame.

Mrs Duggery ushered Ash forward. 'Now, come you on – put that magic stone a yorn down here, in the middle a' the floor.'

Ash pulled the stone out of her jeans pocket and laid it on the floor.

'Now, Flame, can yer put the plan underneath it, please,' said Mrs Duggery.

Flame drew out the plan from the magic box she had carried up, and placed the open plan on the floor beneath the stone.

'Right, thas ready then,' muttered Mrs Duggery. 'Now we

got ter get in ter our positions.' She waved her hand towards the Sprite Sisters. 'You four girls know where ter stand.'

Flame walked to the east side of the tower wall, the direction that represents Fire and Spirit. Marina walked to the south side, the direction that represents Water and Emotions. Ash moved to the position of the west, the place of Earth and Body, while Ariel stood in the north, the direction of Air and Mind.

Standing against the wall, they looked at the tiny old lady in the lilac knitted hat and big brown boots. 'Awright?' she asked. The Sprite Sisters nodded.

Mrs Duggery looked at Verena. 'Now, Verena,' she said. 'You stand there, please, between Ariel an' Flame – in the direction of the north-east.'

Verena bounced into position, a happy smile on her face.

'Tha's the Place of Action,' said Mrs Duggery, fixing Verena with her glinty smile. 'Yer standin' there cause your power, that represent moving in ter life. You understan'?'

Verena nodded. 'Yes,' she replied. 'That's what Flame said.'

Marilyn Sprite and Glenda Glass waited, a little awkwardly, at the south side of the tower. Marilyn was feeling awkward because her magic power had faded many years ago, and she was not sure she would be much help to this circle.

Glenda Glass was feeling awkward because it was the first time in her life that she had worked with other Sprites – and used her magic within the Sprite Code of Honour. No dark magic today, she thought. That's all over now.

'Right, Marilyn,' said Mrs Duggery, pointing. 'Now you got ter stand over here, between Flame and Marina – in the direction of the south-east. Thas the Place of the Ancestors.

You represent all the wisdom the family has learned over time.'

'Okay,' said Grandma, getting into her position. She stood with the wall behind her and smiled at Marina, then at Flame.

'Now Glenda, you got ter stand in the direction of the south-west, between Marina and Ash.'

'The Place of the Dreams,' said Glenda, in a soft voice.

'Thas right,' nodded Mrs Duggery. 'You hold the dreams fer the family.'

As Glenda stood with her back to the tower wall, she remembered the dream she had dreamed the previous night – and she smiled to herself.

Nothing happens by chance, she thought. Everything is connected. That's what Arthur and Lily and Sidney and Mim – and all the other magical Sprites – have always said.

Everything is connected, she thought, wiping away a small tear. You get back what you give out. Now is my time to help to put back the dreams into the family . . .

'Now, that leave me,' said Mrs Duggery, clumping towards the position of the north-west, to stand between Ash and Ariel.

'What does your direction represent, Mrs Duggery?' asked Verena.

'Thas the Place of the Great Laws,' she said. 'The Universal Laws.'

'What are they?' asked Verena.

'Well, there's a number on 'em,' said Mrs Duggery. 'The ones yer got ter think about today, are the Law of Balance. That mean we have to find a middle way. Then there's the

Law of Choices: that mean we have ter take responsibility for our lives an' the choices we make. The Law of Process – thas about taking one step at a time. The Law of Unity – thas about us all being connected ter one another. See?'

Verena nodded. 'Yes – thank you.'

'Now let's get on, then,' said Mrs Duggery.

Silence filled the tower room. Everybody drew a deep breath and stood up straight.

'Are yer all ready?' asked Mrs Duggery.

'Yes,' they all replied.

'Well, I want yer all ter take two steps ter the left,' said Mrs Duggery.

Ariel, Verena, Flame, Grandma, Marina, Glenda, Ash and Mrs Duggery all stepped sideways.

'Now take one step forward, away from the wall,' said Mrs Duggery.

Everyone stepped forward into their new position. The circle they formed was now slightly smaller and had shifted sideways.

'Good,' muttered Mrs Duggery, looking round at them all. 'Now put out yer hands and let the magic flow.'

CHAPTER NINETEEN

THE CROSSED CIRCLE

THE EIGHT Sprites straightened their arms, lifted their hands slightly and turned out their palms.

In the centre of the oak floor – which spanned ten metres across – sat the magic stone on top of the secret plan.

Then Mrs Duggery said, 'The secret plan has led us here today and there are things we need ter do. I want you ter focus yer minds on creating the Crossed Circle on the plan. When we create that, we'll be able ter restore the balance in the whole Sprite family, past and present – and future. Some of the Sprites with magic powers have forgotten the Sprite Code of Honour and they been usin' dark power. They been usin' their power ter hurt people and ter get what they want. That int what our magic power is for. When we restore the balance, these Sprites will come back to using their power only fer good. The dark magic thas been in one part of the family will disappear. The Sprite family will be whole again and the magic will be much stronger.'

Flame looked across at Glenda and noticed her sisters were, too. Verena was gazing at her anxiously. But Glenda's gaze was down at the floor and she seemed to be concentrating hard.

'Now close yer eyes and focus yer minds,' said Mrs Duggery.

The eight Sprites stood silent as they did this.

After a while, Mrs Duggery said, 'Now open yer eyes and hold out yer hands towards the magic stone.'

Everyone opened their eyes and looked at the stone sitting on the plan. As the powerful magic of the Sprites whooshed through the hands of the eight females, the whole tower room filled with a bright white light.

Ariel looked up and around, thinking how pretty the light was, then down again at the stone. It had begun to emit a pulsing blue light and was getting brighter by the second.

Then – *whoosh* – just in front of the Sprites flashed a line of blue light like a neon tube. As it ran clockwise to form a circle of blue light, everyone gasped. Even Glenda looked amazed. Within an instant, the circle of blue light had formed in the tower room. Its brightness and colour matched the magic stone sitting in the centre.

'Keep yer magic flowing,' said Mrs Duggery. 'And focus now on bringing the circle to the centre.'

As she said this, eight lines of bright blue light started to appear inside the rim of the circle – one by one. As these lines of light moved towards the magic stone in the centre of the circle, they looked like the spokes on a wheel.

Within a second, the eight Sprites found they were each standing just outside one of the eight sections of the Crossed Circle. None of them touched the light that ran in front of them.

I wonder if the circle will form above and below, thought Flame.

As this idea ran through her mind, Mrs Duggery said, 'Now visualise bringin' the circle up ter a point above the magic stone, high up – the same distance as the circle to the stone. Then visualise bringin' it down, ter a point below the stone at about the same distance. We're goin' to form a ball of light. Now focus yer minds and let yer magic power *really* flow.'

Flame stood straight, focused. The power coursing through her hands felt stronger and stronger by the second.

I've never felt it like this before, she thought. The power feels *so* strong, and it's different somehow. It's as if it's a new kind of power . . .

She looked round at the other Sprites. How amazing to be standing together like this, she thought. We're all working together. There's no dark magic here.

She looked across the tower room at Glenda and noticed the intense expression on her face. She's as bowled over by this as we are, thought Flame.

'Wow!' squeaked Ariel, interrupting her thoughts.

'Look at that!' cried Ash, her face craned up.

As Flame looked up, she saw that a huge dome of golden light was beginning to form above them.

'And down there!' said Verena.

The wooden floor seemed to have disappeared. Instead, the neon blue lines of the Crossed Circle seemed to stand on an invisible glass floor. Looking down, Flame saw that beneath the circle was an upside down dome of pale gold light.

It's formed a golden ball of light, she thought. Beyond this was bright, white light.

'Incredible!' said Ash, looking up, then down.

'Good heavens!' exclaimed Grandma.

'It's *beautiful*!' whispered Verena.

Glenda gasped and drew a sharp breath. I'm so glad I am here to see and share this, she thought.

Mrs Duggery looked round at them and smiled her glinty smile. 'Now keep yer focus, all a you,' she urged. 'Keep yer power flowin' and send the feelin' a love through yer hands.'

They were silent, each gazing at the light and focusing on their magic power.

Then Mrs Duggery said, 'Now I want each a yer ter think about the family: *all* the family. I want yer ask them ter come forward and be with us now, ter share the Crossed Circle and this lovely gold light. Think of as many names as yer can – the living and those who have passed on. Then call ter them ter come an' join us.'

As the Sprites closed their eyes and thought of their family, the golden light grew brighter and brighter.

When they opened their eyes a minute later, the intensity

of the light was dazzling.

Flame stared at the Crossed Circle – and blinked. What was that in the centre?

Somewhere in the brightness, a shape seemed to be forming.

'There's a man standing there,' murmured Flame.

'I can see him, too,' said Verena.

'It's as if he's walking on an invisible floor,' said Ash.

Who is it, wondered Grandma.

The form of the man became clearer. He seemed to be turning – to be watching the Sprites outside the Crossed Circle.

He was a big man with broad shoulders, reddish hair and a jolly, whiskery face. Smartly dressed in a grey suit, he wore the stiff, rounded white collar that was popular in Edwardian times.

Ariel's mouth dropped open in amazement. 'It's Sidney Sprite!' she cried, wanting to run forward to greet him.

'Stand still, Ariel!' said Mrs Duggery, in a firm voice. 'Hold the Circle.'

As if he could hear her cry, Sidney turned, smiled and waved to Ariel.

'He's waving at me!' she cried. Frantically, she waved back with her right hand.

Beside Sidney, the elegant figure of Mim, his wife, appeared. He turned to her and smiled affectionately, as she took his arm. She was wearing a long velvet coat, a long silk Empire-line dress and a wide-brimmed hat with ostrich feathers sweeping up one side. The couple looked as if they had stepped out of the world of 1910. Now they were walking around the edge of the Crossed Circle.

Flame's mouth dropped open in wonder as the figures of her great-great-grandfather and great-great-grandmother walked past.

This isn't the portal – but it is like a portal, she thought. So what is it we are seeing? They seem to be able to see us. Can we talk to them? I don't think so . . .

Flame's thoughts were quickly distracted as new figures appeared in the golden light.

'It's Lily and Arthur!' exclaimed Grandma.

'So it is!' exclaimed Glenda.

Lily Sprite leaned gracefully on the arm of her husband, Arthur, as they walked around the circle. Sidney's father was also a tall man. He had grey hair and a neat, clipped beard and his blue eyes were kindly, though his expression a little stern. He was dressed in a long black frock coat, with a waistcoat and pocket watch. Beside him walked Lily – a small, blue-eyed, black-haired woman, wearing a rose pink lace dress with the mutton sleeves that were popular around 1890. The great-great-great-grandfather and great-great-great-grandmother of the Sprite Sisters and Verena smiled out at the Sprites standing around the circle of light.

They waved back, smiling.

'Lily is tiny beside him!' laughed Ash.

'How amazing to see them!' exclaimed Marina.

'Can they see us and hear us, Mrs Duggery?' asked Ariel, looking round to her right.

'They can see us, but not hear us,' said Mrs Duggery.

'It's wonderful just to see them!' said Verena.

And how incredible, thought Flame, that I can see these figures – yet still see *through* them to see Ash clearly, at the other side of this circle.

'Look!' cried Ariel. 'There's George Sprite!'

Other figures were beginning to appear in the golden light. First, the handsome figure of George, wearing the army uniform of the First World War. Then came Fred, the Sprite Sisters' great-grandfather and the elder brother of George. His hair was the same deep copper colour as Flame's. Beside him walked Anne, whose warm brown eyes looked just like Ash's. A fine-looking couple, Anne and Fred seemed to have stepped out of the 1920s.

Glenda raised her hand to cover her mouth, as a dark-haired woman in a 1940s dress waved at her. 'There's my mother, Harriet!' she cried in surprise. A look of happiness and sadness passed over Glenda's face and she wiped away a tear.

'Look – there's Margaret Sprite,' said Marina, seeing the figure who had haunted Sprite Towers a few weeks ago, but whose ghost had now been laid to rest.

'And my mother, Elisa and my father, George,' said Mrs Duggery, with a soft smile. 'Ah . . .'

'And my mother Grace,' murmured Grandma. 'And my grandmother, Alice – Sidney's sister! They're waving at me!'

'It's wonderful!' exclaimed Glenda.

The eight Sprite females, standing in the West Tower at the edge of the Crossed Circle, gazed in awe.

'Keep yer minds focused and the magic flowin',' urged Mrs Duggery.

Soon, the ball of golden light filled with Sprites of all ages and generations. Small Sprites, tall Sprites, thin Sprites and fat Sprites; Sprites with dark hair and Sprites with fair hair promenaded around the Crossed Circle. Little Sprite children ran in and out between the grown-ups. Old Sprites leaned on their walking sticks. Young Sprite couples walked arm in arm.

At the centre, George Sprite hugged his brothers and sisters and Margaret hugged her brother, Sidney.

And when the youthful form of Sheldon Sprite appeared and waved at Grandma, she wept. It's him, she thought. It's my darling husband.

Glenda smiled across at her. Marilyn returned her smile and nodded in acknowledgement.

The four Sprite Sisters gazed their handsome, dark-haired grandfather.

'I *do* look like Grandad!' said Marina. 'He's got the same curly hair!'

For a while, the Sprites were silent, each absorbed in their own thoughts.

Then Mrs Duggery said, 'Now we have ter do the healin' and restore the balance in the family. Now listen up.'

The seven other Sprites looked over at the tiny old lady in the lilac knitted hat and waited attentively.

Mrs Duggery's dark eyes glinted as she stared at the figures moving in the ball of golden light. With her ancient magic, she knew what each of the Sprites was thinking and feeling through time and space.

'Thas time ter restore the balance,' she said. 'Now think of us all connecting together – *all* of us, past and present and future. See the lines of magic power runnin' between all a them and all a us. Thousands a connections, millions a connections. What affects one, affects us all.'

As she said this, the ball of golden light filled with lines of blue light connecting the Sprites on the outside of the Crossed Circle with the Sprites on the inside. Hundreds of thousands of light lines ran between each of the Sprite figures in the ball of light – from head to head, heart to heart.

'Look at *that*!' cried Marina.

'*Whoa!*' cried Ariel, looking down at the lines of blue light that joined at her heart. 'The blue light is connecting me to everyone!'

'It's like a matrix!' exclaimed Flame.

'Lines of magic power joining form and time and space,' said Verena, her eyes wide.

'Exactly,' said Mrs Duggery, whose power gave her the vision to see every connection, every beam of light. '*Everything* is connected. *Everyone* is connected. What yer give out yer get back – and *nothing* happens by chance.'

The Sprites stood in silent awe.

'Now focus yer minds on the perfect flow and the perfect balance that makes for harmony,' said Mrs Duggery.

For the next minute, the eight Sprites brought all their power to the feeling of harmony. As they did this, each of them felt a wonderful sense of warmth flowing through their body.

I feel completely peaceful, thought Flame. It's a lovely feeling.

A moment later, Mrs Duggery said, 'It is done.'

As she said this, the figures vanished. The Sprites found

themselves looking at the empty ball of golden light.

'It's incredible – they've all gone,' murmured Ash.

Marilyn Sprite and Glenda Glass looked over at each other and laughed. Whatever magic either of them had experienced in their lives, nothing came close to this.

'Now I begin to understand,' said Glenda.

Marilyn shook her head in amazement.

Mrs Duggery smiled her glinty smile as the golden light faded and the neon blue lines of the Crossed Circle began to disappear.

Within a few seconds, the West Tower room was empty, save for the eight Sprites standing around the wall – and the plan and the stone, still sitting in the centre of the oak floor.

The Sprites stood in stunned silence. The pale winter light was fading. The air was cooling fast. As each of them shivered, it brought them back to the 'real' world.

'Ooh, it's so cold up here,' said Marina, rubbing her hands up and down her arms.

Verena shuddered with cold. 'I'm freezing,' she said.

'So am I', agreed Grandma.

'How long have we been up here?' asked Flame, looking round.

'It feels like ages,' said Grandma, who was feeling a bit stiff.

'A while, thas fer sure,' said Mrs Duggery, walking forwards. She bent down to pick up the magic stone and the plan. Then she held out her hand with the stone to Ash, 'Here yer are, my dear. Well done.'

Ash took the stone and leaned forward to give Mrs

Duggery a hug. 'Thank you so much – that was amazing,' she said, with her warm smile.

Mrs Duggery turned to look at Flame, whose face had a dreamy look. As she handed her George's secret plan, Flame took it and carefully folded it. Then she gave Mrs Duggery a hug and thanked her. 'That was the most amazing experience of my life,' she said.

'You won't forget it,' said Mrs Duggery.

One by one, each of the eight Sprites hugged and thanked one another.

As Flame moved forward to hug Glenda, they both hesitated – then laughed.

'Thank you for joining us and sharing the Crossed Circle,' said Flame.

Glenda smiled. 'I am honoured to have been a part of it,' she said. Then she turned to thank Mrs Duggery. And when she hugged the tiny old lady in the lilac knitted hat, tears flowed down her face. 'Thank you so much, Violet,' she whispered.

Then it was time to hug Marilyn Sprite. Everybody watched, as the two older women – who looked so much alike – gave each other a warm hug and wiped away their tears.

Flame, Marina, Verena, Ash and Ariel joined arms together in a group hug, giggling and jumping up and down.

'We did it!' they shouted. 'We created the Crossed Circle!' They linked arms with Mrs Duggery, Grandma and Glenda, and stood in a circle, laughing and smiling.

'We did it!' they shouted, their breath now forming mist in

the icy air of the West Tower.

'Come on, let's go down before we freeze to death up here!' said Ariel, her teeth suddenly chattering with cold.

'Come you all on, then,' said Mrs Duggery, clumping towards the rickety wooden door. 'Let's go down an' warm up.'

'Time for some chocolate biscuits,' said Ariel.

'Thas right, my girl!'

Ariel laughed. 'So, have we found the treasure?'

'Certainly have,' said Mrs Duggery with a glinty smile.

'Family harmony,' said Flame.

'Thas *real* treasure,' said Mrs Duggery.

CHAPTER TWENTY

THE
RETURN

THE FIVE girls raced down the wide mahogany staircase, whooping. By the time Grandma, Glenda and Mrs Duggery reached the kitchen, the girls had huddled around the warm Aga.

Ten minutes later, the whole family was sitting around the table eating lunch.

Despite the magic she had just shared, Glenda Glass felt awkward to be sitting at the Sprites' kitchen table. She noticed that, while Mum and Dad were unfailingly kind and polite to her, they, too, looked a little awkward. Thankfully, Mum's delicious homemade bread and soup warmed her up – and she found herself feeling very hungry.

If I just sit here quietly nobody will notice me, she thought.

Verena sat next to her and smiled reassuringly.

'You must have been freezing up there,' said Mum, cutting herself a piece of cheese and passing the cheese board on to Glenda.

'Flame warmed the air up for us,' said Ariel, in her matter-of-fact voice through a mouthful of bread.

'But it was freezing again when we finished the magic,' added Ash.

'How long were we gone?' asked Marina.

'You went up just after ten – and it's now half past twelve,' said Mum. 'So tell us what happened, then!'

With lots of gleeful banter, the Sprite Sisters and Verena told the story of the Crossed Circle. Mrs Duggery, Grandma and Glenda listened, catching each other's eyes and laughing. Mum and Dad listened, in various stages of astonishment and wonder.

Everybody had second helpings of soup that day and by the end of the meal, Glenda was feeling more relaxed than she could ever remember feeling, but her mood was tinged with sadness. The Sprites were a lovely family – she could see that – and she wondered why she had ever tried to hurt them.

Ever quick to sense how people are feeling, Mum responded warmly. She realised that Glenda would probably be wondering what to say to Stephen and Zoe – who would be back now in an hour.

We need to get her on her own, she thought.

'Why don't you girls go off while we have some coffee,' suggested Mum.

Verena's face was bursting with excitement. 'Not long

now!' she said. She looked across at Glenda – who smiled at her and said, 'Go on.'

The five girls charged out of the room and through to the library, followed by Archie.

Mum, Dad, Glenda, Grandma and Mrs Duggery sat at the kitchen table with their coffee, enjoying the sudden peace and quiet.

Then Mum looked across at Glenda and said, 'Have you decided whether to say anything to Stephen?'

Glenda looked utterly miserable. 'I don't know what to do,' she said, in a very quiet voice. 'I am worried Stephen will never speak to me again if he finds out about the dark magic, as he'll be so ashamed of me.'

They waited, silent, as this thought hung in the air.

Then Glenda looked at Mum and said, 'I understand that you and Colin had a hard job accepting the girls' magic. Imagine what Stephen would say if he knew what I had done with mine.'

Mum looked down at the table and leaned forward on her arms. 'Hm, I understand your dilemma,' she murmured, thoughtfully. 'On the one hand, this is the time for everyone to be open – that's part of the healing. On the other, what purpose would it serve for Stephen and Zoe to know?' She turned to Dad. 'What do you think, Colin?'

He looked across at Glenda. 'I think a lot has happened and some huge changes have been made in the last few days,' he said. 'There's another big change about to happen for you at The Oaks with Zoe's return. With that in mind, perhaps this is not the right time to bring up the magic and your story.

If I were you, I would wait. You're bound to feel better and stronger when things have settled – and you can choose the right time.'

Marilyn Sprite nodded, then looked at Glenda. 'I agree with Colin,' she said. 'A lot has happened. You're feeling very shaky – and so is Verena. I should let it be for now.'

Glenda wiped a tear away from her cheek and nodded, all the time looking down. 'Yes,' she said, quietly. 'That sounds like wise advice. I appreciate your kindness.'

Mum reached over and touched her arm. 'You need to talk to Verena and agree it between you,' she said.

Glenda looked at Mum, registering this thought. 'Yes, I'd better do that now before Stephen and Zoe arrive,' she said, getting up from her chair. 'We have talked about it – but we'd better make sure we agree.'

'Well, why don't you have a chat to her in the library,' suggested Mum, also getting up. 'It's nice and warm in there and the girls can come in here and help us get cleared up.'

Glenda followed Mum through to the library, where Mum asked her daughters to come through to the kitchen. For the next half hour, Dad, Ash and Ariel cleared up in the kitchen, while Mum, Grandma, Marina and Flame went through to the dining room to set the table for Christmas lunch. Mrs Duggery rested on the Windsor chair beside the Aga with Pudding on her lap and Bert at her feet.

When Mum came back to the kitchen, she said to Dad, 'I was thinking it was just as well that my parents haven't come this year from France. I can't imagine what we would have said about the magic and the Crossed Circle to them – and the girls wouldn't have been able to do this magic.'

Dad laughed. 'Just as well that they're spending Christmas with your brother, then!'

Mum smiled at him. 'You were right, love – about the magic. I didn't need to worry so much. And I'm very glad that things are healed between Glenda and your mother.'

'Yes, it's been an interesting – and rather wonderful – experience,' agreed Dad. 'Charles would have liked to have been here.'

'Yes, it's a shame he's spending Christmas with his parents this year,' said Mum. She turned to look towards the kitchen door. 'I wonder how Verena and Glenda are getting on?'

'We'll know soon enough,' said Dad.

When Verena and Glenda emerged from the library, their faces were streaked with tears – but their expressions were ones of happiness.

'We've agreed not to say anything to Stephen and Zoe about the magic for the time being,' said Glenda. 'And we should be very grateful if none of you mention it either.'

'Of course not,' agreed Dad.

'That's wise,' said Grandma.

'And I've apologised to Verena for being such a rotten grandmother,' said Glenda. The expression on her face showed that she was not joking.

There was a momentary silence, then Verena smiled at Glenda. 'But not any more,' she said.

Mum, Dad and Grandma breathed a sigh of relief.

'That's wonderful!' said Mum. 'I'm so pleased you have

things sorted. Now relax and enjoy your Christmas.'

'Mummy and Daddy will be here any minute,' said Verena. 'I must go and wash my face!' She laughed as she ran off to the cloakroom.

A few minutes later, when Stephen and Zoe's car pulled up to the front of Sprite Towers, Verena opened the front door and charged out to greet them. Everyone followed her – and everyone shed a tear as they watched Verena's joyful reunion with her mother.

'I'm so happy for them,' sobbed Ariel, holding Mum's hand.

'So am I,' sobbed Mum.

Dad sniffed several times then coughed loudly and shook hands with Stephen.

Little Archie jumped up people's legs and then rushed off over the grass to find a stick to carry round in his mouth. Nobody noticed when he carried this into the house and took it behind the drawing room sofa.

Christmas Eve was spent around the kitchen table and the drawing room fire. Mum and Grandma had cooked a delicious meal of smoked salmon, roast beef and syllabub. Everyone tucked in with relish.

'You are the most wonderful cooks!' said Stephen, raising a glass to Grandma and Mum.

They laughed together. 'We enjoy it!' said Grandma.

Zoe looked radiant and relaxed. Like her daughter, she had long blond hair and blue eyes. Stephen kept smiling at her and Verena looked happy.

Glenda watched her family – a little nervously at first –

then with more confidence.

Stephen looked relieved to see that the tension between his mother and daughter that Verena had described a few weeks before seemed to have vanished.

The Sprite family were all in good cheer. Everyone enjoyed the evening.

It was only when Mum discovered the horrible mess that Archie had made with his chewed stick behind the sofa that tempers frayed for a minute or two. Otherwise, all was peaceful at Sprite Towers.

By mid-evening, the Glass family decided to return to The Oaks to unpack and get some much-needed rest. While Grandma, Marina, Ash and Ariel finished setting the dining room table for the formal Christmas Day lunch, Dad and Mrs Duggery cleared up the kitchen and Mum and Flame stuffed the turkey on the table.

When the huge bird was ready, they lifted it into a massive roasting tin and covered it with foil. Then Dad lifted it into the Aga oven, where it would cook, very slowly, all night long.

At ten o'clock Ariel, Ash and Mrs Duggery went up to bed. Half an hour later, Mum, Dad, Grandma, Flame and Marina got into the big red car and drove to the village church for Midnight Mass.

The ancient church was lit by candlelight that evening and the atmosphere was peaceful. When the service finished, they shook hands with the vicar, who was standing by the open door. 'Merry Christmas, Reverend Hodges, and thank you,' said Dad.

'See you in the morning,' said Mum.

As the Sprite family walked out into the crisp night air, they wished their neighbours and friends a happy Christmas.

Then it was back up the long driveway to Sprite Towers. That night the full moon shone brightly over the big house.

One by one, the Sprites said goodnight to Sidney Sprite and made their way up to bed.

As the cold night air moved through the roof of the old house, the timbers settled and creaked. When the last Sprite fell asleep, Sprite Towers gave up a contented sigh and all was still.

CHAPTER TWENTY-ONE

CHRISTMAS AT SPRITE TOWERS

CHRISTMAS DAY dawned sunny and bright and everyone was up early. Dad lit the fires in the drawing room and dining room and soon Sprite Towers was filled with the aroma of wood smoke as well as roasting turkey.

It smells like Christmas, thought Flame, as she came down the stairs.

In the corner of the drawing room, the Christmas tree twinkled. Underneath it were piles of presents that the family would open after lunch.

It was 'all hands on deck' that morning. Whilst Ariel and Ash took care of the animals, Flame helped Mum to baste the turkey again. Grandma laid out dozens of small mince pies and sausage rolls to warm on a tray in the oven, while Marina and Dad were busy getting out bottles and glasses and making a fruit punch. The only person who had not yet appeared was Mrs Duggery.

'I want you all ready by eleven,' said Mum to the Sprite Sisters. 'No jeans today – smart clothes, please.'

Sure enough, at eleven o'clock everyone was ready. Mum was wearing an elegant black dress. Grandma wore a light blue silk dress. Dad wore a shirt and tie. The Sprite Sisters wore colourful skirts and tops.

Flame and Marina had put on the tiniest bit of make-up and hoped Mum would not notice. Mum did notice, but she said nothing. Dad noticed too – and winked at them.

'Shh, Dad,' they giggled.

'Where's Mrs Duggery?' asked Ariel, looking round.

At that moment, the kitchen door opened – and in walked the tiny old lady. Today there was no lilac knitted hat. Her long white hair was drawn into a small bun at the nape of her neck. Though her dark eyes still glinted, she suddenly seemed to look very, very old.

'Mrs Duggery!' cried Ariel, running up to her. Everyone wished the tiny old lady Happy Christmas and kissed her on the cheek.

Then Mum stood beside Mrs Duggery and said, 'Listen, girls, there's something we have to tell you.'

Dad walked forward and stood the other side of Mrs Duggery. A tall man, she came about halfway up his chest in height.

The Sprite Sisters looked at one another with expectant faces.

Dad coughed, then said in a rather formal voice, 'We have invited Mrs Duggery to come and live with us at Sprite Towers. We would like to look after her – and we hope you will be pleased.'

A great whoop of delight went up in the kitchen.

'Fab fantastic!' shouted Ariel.

'Brill!' said Ash.

Flame moved forward to kiss the old lady again. 'I'm so pleased,' she said.

Mrs Duggery's glinty smile softened. 'I thank you all,' she said.

Soon after this, the guests started to arrive for Christmas Day drinks. First were the Glass family, who would be staying on for lunch. Stephen carried in a box of champagne bottles. Glenda and Verena each carried a huge bag of brightly wrapped parcels. Zoe came in with her arm still in a sling.

Next to arrive were Brian and Virginia Blenkinsop, known to the girls as 'Batty' and 'the Gargoyle' on account of his being a 'mad' headmaster and her terrifying face. Then the vicar, Reverend Hodges, and his wife, Gail, came with their children, followed by Grandma's old school friend, Joan, and their bridge-playing friends, Kenneth and Maude James.

It was the McIver family that Flame was waiting for. It felt like an age since she had seen Quinn. The dark-haired, dark-eyed boy always made her heart beat faster – but he seemed to like Verena, too, and Flame was never quite sure who he preferred.

As soon as the McIvers arrived, Marina started chatting to

her best friend Janey McIver. As more people came through the front door, Quinn made a beeline for Flame, grabbed her hand and led her out of the drawing room.

When Harry, the farmer, and his wife Charlotte and the children arrived, they were delighted to see little Archie. Harry's dog, Meg, was the mother of the little pup.

'He's grown a lot,' laughed Harry as he stroked Archie's head. 'I can see you're looking after him well.'

Mum laughed and made an exasperated face. 'Archie's chewed just about everything – chair legs, table legs, shoes, his basket. Nothing is safe!'

'That's Labrador puppies for you!' said Harry.

Verena quickly took her father to talk to Harry to ask when Meg's next litter would be ready.

'It would be so nice to have a puppy at The Oaks, Daddy!' she said, with her biggest smile.

Soon the drawing room was full of people talking and laughing. Dad and Mum went round topping up everyone's drinks, while the Sprite Sisters passed around plates of Grandma's mince pies and sausage rolls.

Batty Blenkinsop ate rather a lot of these and when Grandma came past again he took some more and said, 'Marilyn, you make the best pastry I've ever eaten!'

Grandma laughed as the Gargoyle glared at him.

'Happy Christmas, Virginia,' said Grandma.

'Happy Christmas, Marilyn,' said the Gargoyle, through gritted teeth.

* * *

When the drinks party guests departed, it was time for Christmas lunch.

Everybody raced around in a burst of activity.

The dining room was an elegant room with a high ceiling. Around the cream-coloured walls hung portraits of various Sprites. At the end of the room, beside the window, was Mum's grand piano. In the middle of the room, stood the long antique table, the wood shining. Twelve antique chairs were placed around the table.

Each of the place settings had silver cutlery and an array of crystal glasses. The bone china plates they would eat off today were treasured family possessions. Along the middle of the table were small decorations made of holly and ivy, each with a candle burning brightly at the centre.

'It's all so pretty!' said Ariel, as she sat down.

On the sideboard, Dad carved the huge roast turkey. Mum, Flame and Grandma placed on the table dishes of roast potatoes, roast onions, roast parsnips, carrots, Brussel's sprouts, cranberry sauce, bread sauce, stuffing and Mum's special gravy.

When Mrs Duggery stood up to help serve, Mum said, 'Absolutely not, Violet – you sit still!' So Mrs Duggery sat down again and sipped her glass of wine.

Then everyone was served. Dad sat down at the end of the table, opposite Stephen at the other end.

As he sat down, Stephen stood up holding his glass of champagne.

'I'd like to toast the cooks,' he said, 'and say thank you for inviting us to this wonderful feast!'

'It's so kind of you to invite us!' said Zoe, her face shining with pleasure.

'It's wonderful to have you here!' said Ottalie.

'To the Sprite family!' said Stephen, raising his glass.

'To all the Sprites – wherever they are – and a happy Christmas!' said Dad, as everyone stood up and raised their glasses.

As Glenda raised her glass, she looked over at Marilyn Sprite. Marilyn smiled back – a reassuring smile, as she could sense the underlying anxiety in Glenda's gaze.

Only time will tell if Stephen and Zoe are happy to have Glenda living with them, she thought. She will just have to wait and see.

'Right – let's eat!' said Dad, sitting down.

'I'm starving!' said Verena, tucking in.

'So am I!' laughed Flame.

The meal was delicious and the conversation bowled along.

When they were all replete, the plates were cleared. Then it was time for Grandma's Christmas pudding, served with custard and brandy butter. By the time they had all had a helping of this, everyone felt full up.

As the conversation flowed, Colin Sprite looked around the table with a feeling of deep contentment.

The Sprites are a lovely family, he thought – and I'm a lucky man. As he cast his eyes around, he noticed the dreamy expression on his eldest daughter's face. I wonder what she is thinking about, he thought, seeing she was touching her mouth.

Flame Sprite was miles away. As she ran her finger over

her lips, she was remembering the soft touch of Quinn's lips and the smell of him close to her.

It had been a wonderful Christmas, but best of all was the kiss.

No one had seen her. For once, Mum had not called her away, nor Ariel interrupted them. For ten whole minutes they had stood close in the library under a piece of mistletoe that Quinn had brought with him.

Flame Sprite had been kissed at last.

That's real magic, she thought, with a smile.

SPECIAL THANKS

Thank you to all the Piccadilly Press team for their skill, effort and enthusiasm especially Brenda Gardner, Mary Byrne, Margot Edwards, Vivien Tesseras, Melissa Hyder and Victoria Lee, the copy editor. Particular thanks to my whizz editor, Anne Clark, for her sharp eyes and sound judgment. Also to Chris Winn for bringing the Sprite world to life in his drawing and to Simon Davis and Sue Hellard for their striking cover.

Thank you to Emma Parish for her wonderful readings of the Sprite Sisters on the Oakhill Audio CDs; to Antje Keil and her team at Fischer Verlag for the beautiful German editions of the books and to Matthew Johnson and Nick Stone at Starfish for the fantastic Sprite Sister website.

Thank you to Sarah Salmon and Elaine Stimpson at the Norfolk & Norwich Millennium Library, Sue Morgan and Mike Butler at Jarrold's, Angi Kennedy and Keiron Pim at Archant, Louisa Theobald at Norwich Waterstone's, David Makinson at The Holt Bookshop and Henry Layte at The Book Hive. Your support is much appreciated.

Thanks to my parents, Alan and Jane Ebbage, for their support and enthusiasm and also to Rosie, Alex and Hilary. Thank you also to my sisters, Melanie, Beverley and Charlotte and my niece Marina, the first-ever Sprite Sister fan.

Thank you to all my kind friends, particularly Deborah

Shannon, Cathie Bailey, Carol Hollis, Carol Fairhurst, Liz Dittner, Tom and Pam Stuttaford, Peter and Maria Edwards, Bridget Wood, Charlotte Crawley, Diana Alston, Deborah Howell, Jill Gerrish, Arnaud Geanty and Dinah John.

Lastly, my readers – huge thanks to you all and have *fab fantastic* fun with the Sprite Sisters!

Have You Read All The Sprite Sisters Stories?

1) The Circle Of Power

Each of the Sprite Sisters has a magical power related to one of the four elements – Earth, Water, Fire or Air. When Ariel discovers her power on her ninth birthday, their circle is complete. The girls' magic must be kept secret, and used only for good; if not, the consequences could be dire.

The Sprites' big house in the country is full of laughter and sunshine, but a shadow is falling. Everything the Sprite Sisters hold dear will soon be shattered by the arrival of someone who is intent on destroying their power . . .

2) The Magic Unfolds

The Sprite Sisters' home, Sprite Towers, is under threat. The roof is leaking and their enemy, the ruthless Glenda Glass, is determined to have the house for herself.

And tensions are mounting between the girls as they prepare for the most important concert of their lives. Can the Sprite Sisters resolve their differences and summon all their magic powers to save Sprite Towers?